DETECTIVE LAFLEUR MYSTERIES

BY

STEVE ABBOTT AND JOHN FOUNTAIN

O.R.

Firesign

Hot Gold

Old Man in a Hurry

Murder In Moonlight

A Detective LaFleur Novel

JOHN FOUNTAIN

———

STEVE ABBOTT

This is a work of fiction. Names, characters, places, and incidents
are the product of the authors' imaginations or are used fictitiously.
Some actual names are used by permission.

Copyright © 2019 Steve Abbott and John Fountain

All rights reserved.

ISBN-13: 9781674929392

To the pubs and bars of Madison County;
May they stand long and strong

Frustra fit per plura quod potest fieri per pauciora
—William of Ockham, Summa Totius Logicae

Table of Contents

Murder
in
Moonlight

PROLOGUE

2019: MOONLIGHT RESERVE GOLF COURSE MOONLIGHT BASIN, MONTANA

Mike Wilcynski walked into the Moonlight Reserve clubhouse at the break of dawn. He always got an early start on his course inspection rounds.

"Looks like Doc is back in town," he said, as he saw a godawful, pink and yellow hat hanging on his hook in place of the Moonlight cap that he usually wore. "Same old joker."

Well, he thought, as he put on the hat, *nothing for it but to protect my fair, red-haired head, so on it goes.*

He went outside, stopped and looked around as he did every morning, thankful as always to be working in such a beautiful place. The slanting Montana sun had not yet burned the dew off the rolling swales and hummocks of the fairways and greens, leaving them shining, alternately bright and dark in slender patches of light or deep shadow.

He was almost alone on the course, on his first round of inspections before the rush of mid-morning. As he rumbled down the cart path at seventeen, he heard what sounded like a pistol shot, possibly from the direction of Elk Knob, up above him to the west, although sounds travel in hard to determine directions in the valleys. *Must be Sam up there on his property, trying out a new gun*, he thought. *He's really getting into the Western lifestyle.* By the time he got to the bottom of the fairway, he'd already forgotten about it. He stopped near the green, shut the cart down, and stepped out onto the grass.

He loved this time of day: the coolness, the clear air, the Spanish Peaks across the valley rising up in the early light. He especially liked the quiet. Silence surrounded him, blanketing the course like the dew, no sounds other than the occasional chatter of a small mammal, or the distant staccato of a downy woodpecker.

He walked to the green and knelt down, running his hand along the plush grain of bent grass, pleased at the touch. Perfect. He stood up, absentmindedly wiping his hand on his trousers, looking with satisfaction back up the hill to the west.

His thoughts and the morning silence were abruptly broken by what sounded like a sharp clap of thunder, followed by instant, blinding pain. He reached up convulsively, clutching at the pain in his head.

As he fell to the ground, his last sight was of his hands stretched out in front of him, palms glistening, warm, and red.

PART ONE

How It All Started

I first met Dr. Michael Fuentes about six months ago, at the Pony Bar in Pony Montana, on August 18th, 2029.

It did not start out well.

I had been sent by my editor to Pony—I work for The Madisonian weekly newspaper—to research a story. For those of you who are not familiar with Madison County (or even if you are), the Pony Bar is the oldest continuously operating bar in Montana, started in the early 1900's in a building built in 1877, and used variously as a town hall, boardinghouse, and allegedly a "house of ill repute," until a woman named Bert Welch opened the bar. I'd known of Pony for quite some time, had visited the bar, and loved it, and my first thought at my editor's request to go there was that he wanted yet another puff piece about the bar and the town—it has become quite a tourist attraction over the years.

But that (fortunately) was not his intent. I was to interview Dr. Fuentes regarding an incident that had happened over ten years ago, in August of 2019, something that my editor believed had been subject to what can only be termed (his words) "a gigantic coverup." He even went so far as to call it "Pulitzer-worthy." (*As if*, I thought). My editor had gotten a tip, he said, from a friend with connections "in high places" in the newly merged FBI/NSA/CIA that superseded the Department of Homeland security a couple of years ago. All he would tell me was that there was much more to the story than had ever been made public at the time, and this was my chance to shine. Well, not to brag, but I am considered to be quite a good journalist, well-versed in the "five W's" (who, what, when, where and why), and even though I primarily work for The Madisonian now, before I came to Montana I'd had bylines in the New York Times, the Wall Street Journal, and others. So, I began to think this could be something of interest.

The meeting was to take place at the Pony Bar, my editor explained, because that day, August 18th, was the ten-year anniversary of the death—the murder, actually—of a local resident named Doug Soames, and some locals were holding an informal memorial. Now it suddenly didn't sound all that promising again, since, let's face it, small-town murders seldom win prestigious journalism awards, or even increase readership all that much. Too common. But I agreed not to prejudge and headed off to Pony.

Like I said, the first meeting with Dr. Fuentes was not what I would call auspicious, and nearly made me give up on it before I even got started. Fuentes was nice enough, as far as that goes—polite, even amiable, but extremely close-mouthed. In fact, if it hadn't been for his friend Mary, I wouldn't be telling this story at all.

The story, as I mentioned, takes place ten years ago, in the late summer of 2019. To differentiate between that time and this (that is, August of 2029), I have used different fonts; my present-time interjections are shown in this typeface, while all of the events from 2019 are shown in another. I hope this helps you, dear reader, from becoming disoriented by the jumps back in time.

One other small caveat: many of the events recounted here have been dramatized (and in some cases, reconstructed) to lend the story a more narrative feel, but everything I describe is factual, based on extensive first-person interviews with the principals involved, or on related documentation; in some cases, even real names have been used (by permission).

And the story did turn out to be a pretty good one, after all.

Let's Get This Thing Rolling

THE PONY BAR
PONY, MADISON COUNTY, MONTANA

Based on my editor's description, I recognized Dr. Fuentes immediately—he was standing at the far end of the bar, apparently waiting on an order. He was darkly handsome with thinning, dark hair that must have been rather thick and curly at one time, with an attractive physique for his age, broad-shouldered and fairly trim, though I have to say I thought he would be taller. He also reminded me of the older James Taylor (in fact, I wouldn't be surprised to learn later that he had actually been mistaken for the singer once or twice). As I made my way through the crowded room, he took a pitcher of beer from the bar maid and carried it to a small table against the back wall, where he joined an elderly woman seated there in a wheelchair.

As I edged closer waiting to introduce myself, I couldn't help but overhear their conversation.

"Ten years ago, today. A long time," said Fuentes.

"Oh, I don't know, Doc" the woman replied. "Even at my age, looking back always seems shorter than trying to look ahead. I think it's because the future is so uncertain; time sort of stretches out that direction, and the past seems to bunch up. It just doesn't seem like ten years to me."

She shifted in her wheelchair and reached for her glass of beer; Fuentes did the same. There was now a partial pitcher of beer on the table along with three empty glasses. She looked over at Fuentes, the bright lights on the gaming machines and neon beer signs lining the wall opposite the bar glistening in her eyes. "Here's to Doug," she said, hoisting her glass in the air. She adjusted the oxygen hose under her nose and took a large swig. "This is number two, Doc. Could be my last for the day."

"You always say that, Mary," Fuentes replied, raising his glass in return. "But—and I say this as a medical professional—in my qualified opinion, you are going to make it at least to your traditional number four before the day is over."

As Fuentes put down his beer, I moved behind him. "Excuse me?"

"Yes?" he said, glancing up with what I took to be a slightly annoyed expression.

"Dr. Fuentes?"

Fuentes hesitated a moment before replying, "Yes, I'm Dr. Fuentes."

"Hello. My name is Reagan Collins, for The Madisonian. I was hoping I could talk with you."

"What about?"

"My editor sent me up here to do a follow-up on an old story. A rather interesting story, he said, but one that apparently has never been fully related."

"Okay," Fuentes said, carefully, "one, how did he know I'd be here, and two, just what did he tell you?"

"He'd been told that there was going to be a memorial gathering here this afternoon, and that you would certainly be here, as one of the principals involved in the story," I said, frowning. "Other than that, he didn't say much of anything. Just that I should look for you, that there was an incredible story here just waiting to be told. He said the rest was up to me."

"I'm not sure there is anything I can tell you," Fuentes said, glancing at Mary, as if for confirmation. Mary looked back at him with a noncommittal expression.

I stepped back and put my hands on my hips. "I'm going to warn you in advance, Dr. Fuentes," I said firmly, "I can be very tenacious when it comes to a good story. And I've been told this particular story is *very* good."

Fuentes looked like he was holding back a sharp retort, then gave a tight smile. *Here's a force to be reckoned with*, I thought. "Go ahead, pull up a chair," he said, motioning beside him. "But I'm not promising anything."

"Thanks. All I ask is for a chance to ask a few questions."

As I sat down, Fuentes nodded at the woman seated at the table. "This is Mary Callahan."

"Hello, dear," said Mary, holding out her hand. I was surprised at the firm grip; she looked very frail, constantly adjusting her oxygen hose with her thin hands. The skin on her arms was spotted and scarred, paper-thin, almost translucent. "Very glad to meet you," she said, her voice low and warm.

"Same here," I replied.

"So, Ms. Collins," said Fuentes, "what would you like to know?"

"Well, like I said, I've been asked to look into an incident that happened in Pony. A local man was killed here ten years ago, is that right?"

"That was my friend, Doug," said Mary, looking quickly over at me.

"Oh, please forgive me, I didn't mean to offend. When I'm working, I sometimes forget—"

Mary's face softened. "Oh, don't worry, dear, I'm perfectly willing to talk about it. We both are," she added, nodding at Fuentes. "Aren't we, Doc?"

"Sure, Mary," Fuentes agreed, but hesitantly.

"Go on, Reagan," Mary said. I noticed that she called me Reagan right away. I liked that very much; it said a lot about her.

"Alright, thanks," I said, sincerely hoping that with Mary on my side I could get this thing rolling. "This all occurred way before my time, but from what little my editor told me, and what I've learned by reading over the old reports, it seems there was a lot of confusion over what happened up here, and in Moonlight. For example, there was the murder, well, murders, and some kind of a big confrontation at the Moonlight Lodge, but the report is very vague. There is mention of 'extra-jurisdictional' actions by various federal agencies, but again, I couldn't find any specifics."

Fuentes leaned forward and put his hands flat on the table. "Look, I know you've been tasked with this, but there's just nothing I can say about it."

"But if you could just clear up some of the details," I insisted, "that would really help me out a lot."

Fuentes looked over at Mary again, then turned to me and sighed. "No, I'm very sorry, but I can't tell you anything more than what you already know."

"But that's just it, I don't know anything," I said, desperately. "No one does."

"And that's the way it will stay," said Fuentes, firmly.

I looked over at Mary, imploringly. I didn't even have to say anything.

Mary reached out and took Dr. Fuentes's hand. "It's time, Doc," she said, her voice low. "Past time."

"Well, I don't know, Mary..." His voice trailed off.

"No, Doc. It's time to tell everyone what really happened up here."

"What, the whole story? You sure?"

"Listen, Doc. It's been ten years, now. We owe it to all of them, not just to Doug, even though it's his memorial today." She clasped her hands on her lap emphatically. "It's all water under the bridge, Doc."

Fuentes looked down at the table, as if assessing what Mary had just said.

"You're right, Mary," he finally said, looking up. "But not here, not today. Today is for Doug. And Carl and John." I cocked my head expectantly as Fuentes looked back over at me, his expression more open now. "Would you like a beer, Reagan?" he asked.

"Sure, thanks very much."

Fuentes motioned to the bartender. "Another glass, please?" he called out.

After the bartender had placed the glass on the table and Fuentes began to pour, he looked over at me. "Can you meet me around seven o'clock next Wednesday in the bar at the Moonlight Lodge?" he asked.

"I'll double check my schedule, but yes, I think that's okay."

"Good. It started here in Pony, but Moonlight's where it all ended." He pushed the beer over to me.

I picked up my glass. "Cheers." The other two raised their glasses in return.

"Thanks, Dr. Fuentes."

"Oh, just call me Doc."

"Okay, thanks, Doc." I smiled. *Thank you, Mary!*

"I'll arrange access to Jack Creek Road for you," Fuentes continued.

"I can get access to Jack Creek Road?"

"Well, yes. I know access has long been a matter of controversy, but it is still a private road," Fuentes said. "Even with the recent improvements—though there are still some pretty rough spots—the County Commissioners and the Moonlight company like to keep traffic at a minimum for the sake of the wildlife. Elk, moose, bobcats, mountain lions, bear, deer—even the odd wolverine."

"Okay, thanks." I motioned to the three empty glasses on the table. "I can't help asking: why did you ask for a new glass for me? There are several clean glasses already sitting here."

"I can answer that," said Mary, quietly. "These three empty glasses, they're here in memory of my dear friends. One each for Carl and John, who were here in the thick of it, back then, when it all happened, and who have since passed." She paused. "The other glass is for Doug, who was murdered by those, those—" She scowled. "I can't say it. Anyway, this is their celebration."

"Oh, I'm so sorry, Mary," I said. "I didn't intend to intrude on a special time, really."

"No, of course not, dear. I'm glad you're here." She looked at Fuentes, rather severely, I thought. "And glad the whole story will finally come out."

Poet's Corner? How Droll

MOONLIGHT LODGE
MOONLIGHT BASIN, MONTANA

Unsure of the bar's whereabouts, I hesitated just inside the front door of the Moonlight Lodge, admiring the impressive décor. To my left I spotted the reception desk, and walked over. There was a young man behind the desk, with short, light brown hair and a pleasant round face. He was nicely but casually dressed, mountain style, in a green plaid shirt and stylish denims. Before I could say anything, he smiled and greeted me with a friendly, "Hello, Reagan!"

"Oh, hello," I answered, a bit taken aback. "How did you know who I am?"

"Oh, Doc described you to me—tall, athletic, long blonde hair—a true Montana beauty, he said."

I'm not easily flustered but I have to admit this made me blush. And perhaps raised my estimation of Dr. Fuentes a smidgen. "Well, I'll have to remember to thank him for the compliment."

"I'm Justin, by the way," he said as he came around to the front of the desk. "Welcome to the Moonlight Lodge!"

"Thanks. Can you tell me where I can meet—?"

"No worries," said Justin. "Doc's sitting at Poet's Corner, as usual."

"Poet's Corner? I'm confused. This is a bar, right?"

Justin chuckled. "I'll explain. This way," he said, as he came out from behind the desk and led me out of the lobby.

We walked into the bar area, past a large bronze bear on the hearth of the huge fireplace, and under three full-mount mountain goats high up on stone ledges on both sides of the entrance to the bar. Justin stopped just past the entrance. "Let me explain the layout of the bar," he said. "There are three main areas, named by Doc. The corner to the right is called Local's Corner; one of our regular customers sort of reigns there, as 'Chairman Kirby.' To the far left is the Headwaters, or Mahogany Ridge." *I couldn't help wondering, who would name the parts of a bar?* Justin motioned to the area at the other end of the three-cornered bar. "There's Doc over there, sitting at the middle corner of the bar," said Justin, motioning. "It's called Poet's Corner. Doc never sits anywhere else." I looked over and saw Dr. Fuentes (*Doc*, I reminded myself) sitting at the bar chatting with the barman, a handsome, slender man dressed in a Hawaiian shirt. As I looked closer, I could see that the barman's thick, blond hair was showing a few bits of gray.

Justin stepped back and said, "I'll leave you to him."

"Thank you, Justin," I said. I walked over to where Fuentes was sitting.

"Hi, Doc," I said.

"Hi, Reagan," Fuentes replied. "Right on time! Have a seat." I slipped onto a stool next to Fuentes, laying a small notebook and a pen down on the bar as I settled in. "I'd like you to meet Ethan," he continued, "the finest publican in Montana, as well as a participant in the events of ten years ago."

Ethan looked up sharply and exclaimed, "You're really going to tell the tale, aren't you!"

"I told you I would," said Fuentes.

"The whole thing?"

"Yep."

"But even I don't know the whole story!"

"Well, like I said earlier, I'm going to tell Reagan everything. Or to be more exact, tonight I'm going to *start* telling the whole story. But not until Reagan has a drink—you too, if you will, Ethan."

"Sure, it's very quiet today—thanks!" He turned to me. "First, what will you have, Reagan?"

"Gosh, I don't know. What do you recommend?"

"For tonight? Given the occasion I'd say a good bourbon, wouldn't you, Doc? Sort of set the stage?"

"Exactly right, Ethan."

"And you? Another floater?"

"I'd say another floater is necessary, yes," Fuentes replied, pushing his empty glass across the bar.

I turned to Fuentes. "Floater?" I asked.

"My usual drink of choice, Reagan. Allows me to pace myself over a long evening without cutting into the enjoyment. Ethan, can you demonstrate?"

"With pleasure."

Ethan brought a new highball glass out from behind the bar and dropped a few perfectly formed, perfectly clear ice cubes into it. From a small pitcher, he filled the glass close to the brim. "Moonlight water," he said. He then reached back behind him and pulled down a bottle of Famous Grouse Scotch whisky from the shelf. Very carefully, he poured a quarter of an inch of Scotch on top of the water.

"Here you go."

"Thanks."

"Now, Reagan," Ethan said, "any preferences regarding a bourbon?"

"Well, I don't know. That floater looks just perfect. Can I try one of those instead?"

"Of course."

I waited for my drink, then asked Dr. Fuentes, "You said you were only going to 'start' to tell the story. When am I going to get the *whole* story?"

Fuentes raised his glass. "Well, Reagan," he said, "as Steve McQueen said in *Bullitt*, "Time starts now."

I gave him a quizzical look. "What does that mean?"

"It means that it will take some time. Because it all started for me at the downstairs bar at the Bozeman airport. But it ended right here in Poet's Corner."

Drinks with a Ghost

AUGUST, 2019: BOZEMAN AIRPORT
BELGRADE, MONTANA

Fuentes was sitting at the airport bar waiting for a ride home. He was drinking a poorly made floater (really just a Scotch and water, and with the wrong Scotch), when an attractive, fit-looking woman wearing a casual business suit came and looked around for a seat. A bit younger than he was, fortyish, with long coppery-blonde hair and a light complexion, she glanced over uncertainly at Fuentes as she maneuvered her roller bag close to the bar, then sat down next to him; it was the only stool open.

Fuentes turned to her and asked, "Coming or going?"

The woman hesitated, then answered guardedly, "Going." Fuentes looked at her expectantly, encouraging her to go on. "I'm on my way home to Kentucky," she finally said. "Well, not home, exactly; I'm currently working out of Frankfort, Kentucky, and have to report in there first. Then home. But I have quite a bit of time to kill before my flight, so I stopped off here on my way to check my bag. You?"

"Just getting home, also from a work assignment. Waiting for my ride." He looked down at her bag, a small carry-on, black with black wheels, and motioned to his bag sitting next to it. "We all seem to have bags that look exactly the same these days. You said you're checking it, though, not carrying it on to avoid the baggage fee?"

The woman leaned over and pointed to the bar-coded airline label attached to the strap on the back side of his bag. "I see you also checked yours. We must be the only two passengers in the world who check a carry-on bag. I guess most people are in such a hurry they can't stand the thought of waiting for their luggage when they get home. But I've got some work-related items I can't take on board. So, no choice but to check it."

"Same here," Fuentes replied, "but not work-related; just something special for some friends who are visiting." He paused, wanting to prolong the conversation, and then asked, "Was your time in Montana productive?"

"Yes, as a matter of fact," she said. "I believe the company I'm working for will be very satisfied with my report. It hasn't been easy, though. I've been away for over a month. I can't wait to get home to see my daughter, Ailsa."

"I'm sorry, did you say 'Elsa?'"

"Close. It's spelled a-i-l-s-a; the first syllable is pronounced more like 'ail.' It is actually a Scottish form of Elsa, which was my grandmother's name. It originally comes from the Vikings, meaning something like 'elf victory.' I chose it because it has also come to mean something like a spiritual victory, or spiritual strength. I wanted my daughter to have a name that could inspire her." As she talked about her daughter she seemed to visibly relax.

"That's marvelous. How old is she?"

"She just turned nine. It's been very inconvenient, being away. She's just been accepted into a special school—she has some learning disabilities, and has really been struggling, but we're very hopeful about the new school. I really need to be back there right now."

The barman came over and interrupted, asking for her order. "I'll have bourbon," she said. "Do you have any Weller?"

"Sure, several varieties, as a matter of fact."

"Okay, then I've got a special request for you."

"What is it?"

"I'd like a sixty-forty blend of W.L. Weller 12 and Old Weller Antique 107. Straight up, please."

The bartender shook his head. "That's a new one. Well, I'll give it a shot." He turned away, muttering.

Fuentes looked over at the woman. "I know next to nothing about bourbon," he said. "But even as an inveterate Scotch drinker I would say that your request is pretty unusual."

"I suppose so," she admitted, and pointed to his glass. "What's that you're drinking?"

"Oh, just a Scotch and water."

"You know," she said, "the finest bourbons in the world are still made here in the U.S., in Kentucky. But lately the best Scotch is coming out of Japan."

"I'll stick with Scotland."

The bartender returned with her drink. "Here you go," he said, dubiously.

"Thanks very much." She laid a twenty-dollar bill on the bar.

"Be right back," the bartender said.

Fuentes eyed her as she took a small sip of her drink. "Well?" he asked. "Are you going to explain?"

"Pretty good. I think he got it just right." She looked away, apparently distracted by something. "I call it 'Poor Girl's Pappy.' It's almost as good as—"

Before she finished her sentence, she jerked upright, bolted off of her stool, grabbed the carry-on at her feet, and left the bar in a rush, without another word. Fuentes watched in surprise as she ran out the doors and across the road into the parking lot. *She'd said she was on her way to check her bag, hadn't she?* As he watched, two men appeared behind her, following at a brisk pace. *She didn't even finish her drink. Or wait for change. What's going on?*

Just as the three disappeared behind a row of cars, his phone rang.

"Hi, Jamila. Okay, be right out."

Fuentes finished his drink and hopped off the stool, pulling the carry-on bag behind him. Outside, Jamila was already waiting at the curb.

"Hi," he said, throwing the bag into the back seat, then climbing into the car. Behind the wheel was a slightly built, dark-haired woman of indeterminate middle-age, whose porcelain-smooth light olive skin and flashing black eyes made her look much younger than her years. Fuentes leaned over for a quick kiss. "Bad trip down, huh?"

"There are fires everywhere," Jamila said. "Had to follow a pilot car through Gallatin Canyon."

"Hope it's not so bad going back."

The trip from the airport to Moonlight Basin usually takes an hour or so, but when they got into Gallatin Canyon, traffic had been slowed to fifteen miles an hour, with sheriff's deputies deployed every few miles. Fires were burning on both sides of Highway 191, occasionally with large flames. Big Sky was enveloped in smoke. When they finally got to Moonlight, the air was still smoky, but nothing like down below.

"Everyone here?" Fuentes asked Jamila, as they pulled into the garage.

"Inside, anxiously waiting your return."

We're Not Getting Any Younger

MOONLIGHT LODGE

I took a sip of my floater. "You never saw the woman again?" I asked, interrupting the narrative at this point.

"We'll get to that," answered Fuentes. "Be patient."

"Okay, sorry. I told you I was tenacious."

"Yes, you did. Now, where was I?"

"Just leaving the airport. But who was waiting for you when you got home?"

"Oh, yeah, I haven't introduced the rest of the group," Fuentes said. "We had visitors that weekend from Oswego, New York, where I used to live. First, there was A.C. LaFleur—he is a retired police detective—and his wife, Maggie. I've known Maggie for years; she was the head nurse at the Oswego Hospital where I worked. A.C. now owns a restaurant in Oswego, the 1850 House, even though he has semi-retired even from that—it's open only for special catered events now. The third guest was Frank Ivanovich, also known as 'Big Frank,' a close friend of A.C.'s. Quite an interesting character; ex-military, with a varied and somewhat mysterious background. He was the head chef at the 1850 House when it was in full operation."

"And who is Jamila?" I asked.

"A close friend." He amended that immediately. "A very close friend, I guess I should say. She's living with me out here, for the time being, at least. We met in Oswego while helping A.C. on a case. She was a professor of electro-mechanical engineering at RIT, the Rochester Institute of Technology, and is now at SUNY, Oswego."

"So, is it serious?"

"Time will tell, I guess. Jamila is still associated with SUNY and is only here on a three-month sabbatical."

"And what was the case you were involved with?"

"Oh, that's too complicated to go into now. Proverbial long story. Anyway, to get back to the group at the house that weekend:

I'd brought home some special whisky as a celebration, Famous Grouse Smokey Black, in order to toast A.C. and Maggie's wedding anniversary. And to remember an absent friend, someone we called the Professor. Who was central to the case I just mentioned," he added as an afterthought. "And given the trip home, I was also planning to toast to our continuing safety, what with the fires that were all around us." He paused. "You'll hear all about A.C. and Frank. They were heavily involved in the case, as always."

"Okay, thanks," I said. "I'll try to be patient."

After greeting everyone in the living room, Fuentes put down his bag. "I brought something back for you and A.C.," he said to Frank. "It's wrapped in bubble pack, right on top. Open up the bag and get it out while I go change."

A minute later, Fuentes heard Frank shout out to him. "Hey, Doc! Are you sure you want me to open this?"

"I'll be right there," Fuentes called back. "Quit fussing and open the bottle!"

When Fuentes walked into the living room, he was greeted by smiling faces, and everyone holding a small glass of whiskey. Big Frank held his glass high.

"What a wonderful surprise!"

A.C. walked over and reached out his hand towards Fuentes. "Doc, what a fantastic present." Fuentes shook his hand, somewhat bemused.

"Three hundred dollars a shot!' said Frank.

"Six hundred in Hong Kong or Tokyo!" said A.C., shaking his head in wonder. "Frank, where's Doc's drink?"

Frank walked to the bar and brought a glass over to Fuentes, who was still standing there with a confused look on his face. "What are you talking about?"

"Here, drink up!"

Confusion turned to surprise. "Hey. What is this stuff?" he asked, after taking a sip. Blank stares were returned as the group tried to figure out what the problem was. "This isn't Grouse," Fuentes continued. "I brought home Smokey Black." He walked over and picked up the bottle sitting on the bar and looked at the label. "Pappy Van Winkle Family Reserve," he read. "The twenty-three-year-old!

What the hell? This is one of the highest priced whiskies you can buy! People enter expensive lotteries just trying to get their hands on it. What is it doing here?"

I interrupted again. "Sorry, I know I said I'd be patient, but I'm not following this Pappy thing at all." *This group knows way too much about whiskey.*

Ethan leaned over the bar. "Pappy Van Winkle is top of the line bourbon, and the high-end of their product lineup has taken on almost mythical proportions. Like Doc just said, it's very hard to get and very expensive."

"But how could it be that expensive? It's just whiskey, right?"

"Oh, no; Pappy Reserve is the Holy Grail of bourbon, as far as many bourbon drinkers are concerned. Can't get any better. Or rarer. There were only seven hundred and ten bottles produced of the twenty-three-year old, in 1989. Comes in a custom box, made out of the wood from the barrel it was aged in, no less."

"Do you have any?" I asked.

"One."

"Can I ask how much it cost?"

"Let's just say I can turn a profit of about five-thousand dollars on that single bottle, but only because I was lucky enough to get it from the distillery directly. At black market prices I would lose money."

Thar's gold in them thar bottles, I thought, still not quite understanding.

"Another floater, Doc?" Ethan asked.

Fuentes nodded.

"Did you like the Pappy?" I asked Fuentes.

"That's just it," he said emphatically. "You've just asked the sixty-four-thousand-dollar question. A.C. and Frank took big sips and smiled, but by the next sip the smiles were gone. Now, they're staring at each other with perplexed looks. I remember A.C. saying 'this emperor isn't wearing any clothes.' Then Big Frank took the bottle from my hand. Holding it up to the light, he said 'right size, right label, hand-numbered—but wrong taste.' I was still wondering where in hell it came from, but Frank went on. 'Doc,' he said, 'you've brought us a bottle of counterfeit Pappy.' And I looked at him and said, 'Frank, I've never seen this bottle before in my life.' Well, he and A.C just stared back at me. Now they were as confused as I was."

"Yeah, you said you'd brought home something called 'Smokey Black.' Where did the wrong whiskey come from?"

"That's what we were all wondering. I immediately went into the living room and took a look at my carry-on. But it wasn't mine. Very similar in appearance, but not mine. Looking inside, I found another whiskey bottle, but empty and unlabeled, wrapped in bubble wrap, and next to it a clear plastic bag full of little gray marbles, like Chinese Checkers pieces. Then it came to me. A quick look at the clothing lying in the top of the bag confirmed it. The woman in the airport bar. Our bags must have gotten switched when she rushed out."

"And you were left holding the wrong bag!"

"Exactly. And then I remembered the drink she'd ordered at the bar, just before she bolted, a mix of two varieties of Weller; she called it a 'Poor Girl's Pappy.' Is that what we had here? What on earth was she up to?"

Wrong Bag, Wrong Bottle?

DOC'S HOUSE

Putting the bottle of Pappy Van Winkle aside for the moment—the presumably fake Pappy Van Winkle—Fuentes began searching through the carry-on.

"Any ID?" Frank asked.

"Nothing I've found so far, but her luggage tag says Kyla Macdonald, with a Cincinnati address."

"You didn't notice that there was no claim check tag on the handle of your bag when you left the airport?"

"No, I just grabbed it out from under the bar. Then she ran out and my cell rang at the same time. I didn't really pay any attention to it." He sat down heavily on a swivel chair and sighed. "Well, it's too late to go all the way back down to the airport now, especially with fire traffic. I'll drive down in the morning. Maybe she turned in my bag when she discovered the mix-up."

"Yeah, you'll probably be able to straighten it all out tomorrow."

"Hope so." He looked over at the bottle of Pappy Van Winkle sitting on the bar. "At least now I know what she meant by Poor Girl's Pappy," he said. "Pappy Van Winkle. But you say you don't think it's legit?"

"It sure doesn't seem like it. And A.C. agrees."

"It doesn't make sense." He straightened out the contents of the bag and zipped it shut. "Well, I just hope I get the Grouse back."

Doc's Five Minutes of Fame

DOC'S HOUSE

The next morning, Frank made breakfast—homemade scones, fruit, coffee and juice. It was all on the table, buffet style, and everyone had filled their plates and retreated to various locations around the house, or out on the deck, eating and catching up on their tablets and smart phones.

The calm was broken by a loud "Oh, my God!"

Fuentes was sitting at the bar in the kitchen, but his cry had attracted everyone's attention. Frank came in from the deck, and A.C., Maggie, and Jamila all looked up from their chairs in the living room.

"What is it?" called A.C. from the living room.

Fuentes didn't answer, but sat shaking his head. "Oh, my God. Awful. Unbelievable."

Frank leaned over to look at Fuentes's iPad. "What is it?" he asked. By this time, the rest of the group had made their way over to the bar.

Fuentes held up the iPad and began to read, skipping through the article quickly, hitting the high points. "'A woman was found dead in the airport parking lot yesterday. Apparent foul play. Name withheld pending notification of kin. Let's see, not much more, any help appreciated, etc.' And there's a CCTV picture of her, there in the airport bar, with me sitting right next to her!"

Maggie and Jamila had come closer and were craning their necks to read along with Fuentes. There was a shocked silence as the group finished the short article.

"Not much information, other than the bare facts," commented Frank.

"No," said Fuentes. "Damn! I was just this morning thinking about how pleased she'd been at finishing her business successfully. And how anxious she was to get back to her daughter. Damn!"

"We're going to have to get that bag back right away, now," said Maggie.

"Not only that," added A.C., "we need to notify the Gallatin sheriff's department that we have it. And that's really where it has to go, not back to the airport. I'll call them for you."

Fuentes nodded in agreement as he went over and picked up the bag and tried to rearrange the contents a bit. A.C. went to the other room to call the sheriff's department.

After about ten minutes, A.C. returned to the kitchen.

"Here's what they know. They confirmed that her name is Kyla Macdonald," he announced. "She was identified later by a flight attendant. Went to the University of Kentucky—that's why the flight attendant remembered her, apparently, she'd been wearing a UK sweatshirt, and the flight attendant had also gone there."

"Get to the point, man!" said Frank, impatiently.

A.C. was used to Frank's harmless outbursts and calmly went on with his recital. "They say they can't make it up to Moonlight right now, but will want to interview you, Doc, maybe by phone, as soon as possible. The deputy I talked with also said that given the fire situation, and now that she's been identified, there's no real urgency on returning the bag as long as you can send them some photos. They'd like shots of both the bag and the contents."

"Okay, I'll do that now."

"At the moment, they think it was probably a robbery gone bad," A.C. continued. "They'll review the airport CCTV loops, see if anything turns up, but he said the actual murder happened in a section of the lot with lousy coverage." He turned away, shaking his head. "Oh," he said, looking over at Fuentes, "and your bag wasn't found with her, either."

"Whoever killed her took it with them? Thinking it was hers?"

"Apparently," said A.C., "or someone else took it afterwards, which is very unlikely."

"Yeah. Well, I'd better get some pictures for the sheriff and then get this bag repacked." He began laying out items on the dining table, all except the bottle of Pappy Van Winkle they had been sampling the night before, which was sitting over on the kitchen counter and which he'd momentarily forgotten about. Walking over to pick it up, he shook his head sorrowfully. "Damn it all."

A.C. looked over at Fuentes with a searching look. "You seem pretty upset by this."

"Yeah, I suppose so. She didn't have much time before she was startled away, but had started to tell me about her nine-year-old daughter, whose name is Ailsa; I think she said it means 'elf queen,' or something, very cute, anyway. Ailsa has some learning difficulties, she said, and they had just found the perfect school for her." He came back over to the bag and replaced the bottle of Pappy. "And on top of all that, she really impressed me with that drink she ordered. Very classy."

Jamila looked up from her chair by the fireplace, eyebrows furrowed. "Sometimes I have no idea what goes through your mind," she said.

"Me either," he answered, shaking his head again, sighing. "Me either."

I shifted on my stool and leaned in. "What happened then?" I asked. "After you found out the woman had been killed, I imagine you were pretty upset. Didn't you want to get down to Bozeman, find out more about what had happened?"

"No, not really. It seemed pretty clear that nothing was going to happen right away, and after all, even though it was certainly upsetting, it didn't really concern us, other than needing to get the bag back to them at some point. So, we took a hike."

Hmmmm. If I got killed after sitting in a bar next to Doc, I would hope he'd do something more for me than just go for a hike!

Elkhorn Trail

MOONLIGHT BASIN

The air had cleared somewhat overnight due to the shifting winds and it had turned into a beautiful day, even if still a bit hazy.

Elkhorn Trail was to be the New York group's introduction to Montana geography, geology, flora, and if lucky, fauna (although on this trail at this time of day, a moose sighting was unlikely; and as common as bears were in these woods, encounters were sporadic and happened primarily along the roads, as a bear briefly left the cover of the forest while traversing the area.)

Doc had taken some care in preparing Maggie and LaFleur for the hike, providing advance instructions of the type of clothing and foot wear they should bring with them. To that end, they both looked as if they had been born and bred in Big Sky country. LaFleur wore light olive drab hiking pants, a breathable long-sleeved shirt, and low hiking boots; Maggie was similarly outfitted.

LaFleur had recently crossed over to the wrong side of seventy and was still wondering how he'd gotten there in such a short time. Of average height and medium build, with longish gray hair neatly combed straight back, he wore classic (Maggie said old-fashioned) black-rimmed glasses and often sported a Detroit Tigers ball cap (having no favorite team of his own, he had adopted Doc's home town team).

Maggie was a few years younger and somewhat shorter than LaFleur, similarly trim and fit. Her once dark red hair had started to shade into a lighter auburn, touched here and there by a compatible streak of gray. Maggie had introduced Fuentes and LaFleur several years earlier. That introduction had led them to partner on several investigations—usually at the instigation of Maggie—and eventually had led to Maggie and LaFleur partnering in a more intimate manner—they'd moved in together after LaFleur's houseboat had gone up in flames, and had gotten married the year before their visit to Montana.

The last member of the Oswego delegation was "Big Frank" Ivanovich. Fuentes had not worried about trying to prepare Frank for the hike—Frank was always ready for anything.

The Gallatin trail led from the house to the Moonlight Lodge, where they picked up the longer Elkhorn trail, which went up the side of the mountain. After doubling back under the Pony Express ski lift and getting into the forest, Fuentes began pointing out wildflowers—lupine, Indian paintbrush, heart-shaped arnica, and post-bloom glacier lily. After about forty minutes of gradual climbing, they reached the end of the trail, a vantage point where someone had placed a small wooden bench. The large views down the valley and across to the Spanish Peaks were spectacular from up there, and something A.C. and Maggie had not yet experienced.

"Good job, you two," Fuentes said to them, patting each of them on the back. "We're at about eighty-eight hundred feet here, after an elevation gain of around six hundred feet. So, not an extreme hike, but a good workout all the same."

"It's spectacular," said A.C., spreading his arms out, as if to encompass the entire vista. "Simply astounding."

Fuentes edged over to the rim of the small outcropping where they were standing. "That's Fan Mountain straight ahead," he said, pointing, "and over to the right is the Spanish Peaks."

"Why are they called 'Spanish Peaks?'" asked Maggie.

"No one knows for sure," replied Fuentes. "A lot of theories, as usual, but most likely they were named by prospectors coming up from old Mexico. Now, the Tobacco Root range, over there," he continued, gesturing out past the Spanish Peaks to the left, "was named after a local plant – arnica, that plant with yellow flowers we saw down below? An old name for that was tobacco root."

"They look so far away," said Maggie.

"They are," said Fuentes, "but yet they're still in the same county—Madison County is three times the size of Rhode Island, and nearly the size of Delaware."

"What all is down there?"

"All through the Madison River valley there are a lot of farms and large ranches. And some of the best cowboy bars anywhere."

"Now you're talking," said Frank.

Fuentes looked back behind them. "Lone Mountain, back that direction, is over eleven thousand feet. It's a 'young' mountain, less than a hundred million years."

"Old enough for me," said Frank.

Fuentes ignored him and went on with his geology lesson. "Lone Mountain at one time was a volcano, but probably never erupted—although a side may have blown out, like Mt. St. Helens. Geologists always describe the interior of the mountain as a 'Christmas tree' of magma that pushed up through the rocks, creating a 'trunk' and 'branches' of an igneous rock called dacite."

"Okay, now I know more than I ever needed to know about Lone Mountain," jibed Frank.

Fuentes turned to Jamila. "Tell me again, why did we invite him?"

"Because he can cook," she said.

"Oh, yeah. Which reminds me, by the time we get back it will be time for you to start dinner, Frank."

They started back down the trail, everyone glad to have had the distraction and the exercise, feeling revitalized.

Part way down, Frank asked the only question that Fuentes had not been able to answer that day: "Hey, Doc, why is it called 'Elkhorn' trail? Elk don't have horns; they have antlers."

Fuentes sat there silently at the bar for a couple of minutes, as if he were done with the story, while I fidgeted. He leaned back on his stool and looked around for Ethan, waving him over after he caught his eye.

"So, now what?" I finally cried. "Nothing happens, you take a nice hike and then just go back home and have dinner? That's it? What about the bag, the Pappy Van What'sis, the murder, everything?" I tried not to sound too disappointed in the story so far. *This story is lame. My editor is lame!*

Fuentes smiled. "Oh, don't worry. There's more. A lot more. The next day," he said, as Ethan walked up to us, "all hell broke loose."

Slow Ride

MOONLIGHT RESERVE GOLF COURSE

Fuentes had been the first golfer on the course that morning, even beating Mike out of the clubhouse. He had just teed off from the Hammond tee box at seventeen when he heard a gunshot. It had come from somewhere up ahead of him, which was odd—the shooting range was behind him, way back up on the hill, and this hadn't sounded at all like skeet shooting in any case. More like target practice with a large caliber pistol, but just a single shot. He mentally shrugged and started down the fairway, unconcerned. Gunshots were a common occurrence in Montana, even around here.

He'd managed to hit his drive over the ridge today (well, in two shots and from the front tee), so he thought he would get a good roll down the massive hill ahead. Every little bit helped on what was from the back tees a seven-hundred-and-seventy-seven-yard hole.

He crested the hill and looked down the long expanse of hummocks and swales stretching out below him towards the green, looking for his ball. Looking out farther, all the way to the green, he spotted Mike, wearing his bright orange and yellow cap. At the same instant, he heard a second shot, much louder than the first, coming from across the valley, from the direction of Jack Creek Road.

He saw Mike fall to the ground face-first next to his cart, his arms spread out in front of him. He had not even tried to catch his fall.

Fuentes dropped his club and started to run.

The whole time while waiting for the ambulance, Fuentes had stayed with Mike, lying alongside him in the back of the greenskeeper's cart.

The members who had been at the clubhouse when they brought Mike up stayed a respectful distance away, though continually milling about near the door, craning their necks to try to see what was going on. Nick, the head pro, rushed back and forth bringing various items to Fuentes as he asked for them—towels, ice, a blanket.

Finally, they heard the siren. A few moments later, the ambulance pulled up onto the apron next to the clubhouse.

As the EMTs shifted Mike to the gurney and then into the back of the ambulance, Fuentes called the driver over and bent close to his ear.

The driver nodded, then turned away.

Once Mike and Fuentes were situated in back, the ambulance pulled away slowly, made its way through the parking lot, then on up the sinuous road to Moonlight and from there down the hill to Big Sky.

There were no lights or siren.

DOC'S HOUSE

As he stood looking out the main window at the Spanish Peaks, A.C.'s phone rang.

"Hello, Doc. Where are you? We've been back from our hike down to Ulery's for a couple of hours."

"A.C., listen. Something's happened, but I don't want you to react to it when I tell you."

There was a pause. "All right, go ahead."

"Mike Wilcynski has been shot."

Another, longer pause. "Mike from the golf club?"

"Yes. You met him the other day."

"I remember."

"I'm at the hospital in Big Sky. I need you to come down and pick me up."

"Well, sure, I—"

"Don't tell anyone you're coming here. Tell them that my car is over at the club and it won't start, or something. I'll explain after we get home."

"Okay, sure, Doc. I'll be right there."

A.C. slipped the phone into his pocket and walked casually into the living room where everyone had gathered.

"Um, Jamila, can I borrow your car? I've got to run out for a bit," he said. "Doc is stranded—his car is being balky, won't start."

"I'll go, A.C.," said Jamila.

"No, no, that's okay. Anyway, didn't Frank say he needed help with dinner tonight?"

"That's right, Jamila, you said you'd do the Yorkshire puddings and the Pavlova," agreed Frank, without looking up from his magazine.

"Well, okay then, A.C., you go." Jamila walked to the bar, grabbed a set of keys and tossed them to him.

"Thanks. See you in a bit."

It was more than an hour later that Fuentes and A.C. returned to the house, and the commotion that ensued when they came in reached just about the level of chaos they'd expected. Fuentes related only the barest facts, putting everyone off until such time as it was possible to sit down and go over everything calmly. "Cocktail hour," he said. "I'll explain everything. Until then, just relax and let things settle a bit."

Mollified, and with no other choice, everyone went back to what they had been doing—Frank in the kitchen preparing dinner, Jamila reading a book, A.C. out on the deck admiring the Spanish Peaks.

"Maggie," Fuentes said, drawing her to one side, "can you help me upstairs for a minute?"

It had been nearly an hour since Fuentes and A.C. had returned home, and they had all gathered in the living room for cocktails.

"Who on earth would want to shoot Mike?" Jamila asked, half rising from her chair.

"Let me finish telling you what happened first." Jamila sat back down. "Like I said a minute ago, I had nearly caught up with Mike. I was on seventeen when I heard a gunshot, just as I teed off. I didn't think anything about it, and started out onto the fairway. My ball had just cleared the hump, and I expected to see it a long way down on the other side. Then there was another shot. A different sound this time, like a high-powered rifle, in the direction of Jack Creek Road. The first one had sounded more like a pistol. Anyway, it was just as I started down the hill, right after hearing that second shot, that I saw Mike down on the ground. I got down there as fast as could."

Maggie held up her wrist and tapped her watch. Fuentes nodded, and she got up and left the room.

"I immediately saw that he was bleeding profusely," Fuentes continued, watching Maggie climb the stairs. "Blood everywhere. I didn't have time to think about what might have happened, I just grabbed a towel from his cart and tried to stop the bleeding. Once I thought I had him stabilized, I grabbed his radio and called for help. They helped me load him onto his maintenance cart and we drove up to the clubhouse." He stood up and went to the kitchen bar and mixed another floater, talking over his shoulder. "It took quite a while for the ambulance to arrive, as you can imagine. And the trip down the mountain was a slow one." He came back into the living room and sat down heavily.

"The longest trip of my life," he said.

...and Bears, Oh My!

MOONLIGHT LODGE

"You know, Doc, I do know quite a bit about that day," I interrupted. Fuentes gave me a quizzical look. "Oh, nothing official," I said. "My editor told me he'd tried to get the rest of the story from you long ago, but you always just clammed up. So, I did a little digging on my own."

"Go on," Fuentes replied, guardedly.

"It was a head wound."

"That's right. How did you know?"

"I talked to one of the ambulance drivers. Not working anymore, but even after all this time, he still remembers it. All the blood!"

"Well, you know, there can be a lot of blood, even from a superficial scalp wound. It bleeds from both sides, until the heart stops."

I hesitated before continuing, afraid this might be going too far. "The driver also said that while they were loading him into the ambulance, you bent over close to him and whispered something in his ear. He wouldn't tell me what. Maybe, 'goodbye, old friend,' something like that?"

Fuentes shifted uncomfortably in his chair. "Reagan, not now."

"But what did you say to him?"

"Maybe some other time, Reagan. Now, where was I?"

"Wait, there's one more thing. The driver told me that you told them to do a 'slow ride,' he called it, down to the hospital. Why?"

Fuentes picked up his drink and finished it in a single gulp. "Look, it's getting late. Like I said, let's pick this up later, okay?"

I'm going to have to push harder, I thought.

Ethan had come over to the table to clear up moments before, and was standing there waiting to ask if we needed anything more. I turned to him and asked in a formal tone, "Ethan, may we join you again for cocktails tomorrow evening?"

"Of course," he answered, before Fuentes had a chance to respond. "I'm sure Doc is anxious to finish the telling of the tale." He smiled at Fuentes. "The *whole* thing."

Fuentes shrugged, then turned to me and nodded in resignation.

"Fine, it's a date," I said, brightly. "I can't wait for tomorrow's 'floating grouse.'"

Fuentes looked back at Ethan. "Would you mind escorting Reagan out to her car?" he asked. "Oh, and stop at the front desk for a flashlight and some bear spray."

"Bear spray? Is that necessary just to walk to the car?"

"You never know, Reagan," said Ethan. "The bears around here are very unpredictable. The staff even keeps a gun handy behind the reception desk, for worst case scenarios."

"Such as?"

"Well, in the event a bear decides to investigate the inside of the lodge, we have to be prepared. Bears are spotted on the steps and around the back patio and pool all the time. You can never tell what they'll do."

"Okay, let's go! And don't worry, I'll be close behind you! See you tomorrow, Doc."

Please Lord, Not `60s TV!

MOONLIGHT LODGE

As I walked through the parking lot on my way to meet Fuentes, I noticed a small, bright red sports car parked next to the usual assortment of mud-splattered trucks and SUVs. When I got inside, I stopped at the desk and asked Justin about it.

"Who drives the little red Sunbeam?" I asked. "It's so cute! And it's got something painted on the door—*MAXWELL SMART*. What on Earth does that mean?"

"The car is a dead ringer for the one used in the old *Get Smart* TV series. The owner is a member here, and likes to liven things up from time to time. He sometimes takes off his shoe and answers it like a phone."

"Is anything around here normal?" I asked.

"Off hand? Nothing I can think of."

I continued on into the bar, where I found Fuentes in his usual spot in Poet's Corner.

After we had ordered floaters and discussed the Sunbeam, I jumped right in. "So, who was it, Doc? Who shot Mike?"

"Whoa, Nellie, hold on! Where are those finely-tuned investigative reporter instincts you've been displaying so admirably up to now? We need to set the stage before we bring up the lights and raise the curtain."

"Oh, you're right. I've just been thinking about it all day!"

"Never mind, I understand. So, I had just told you about that day at the golf course. Well, the next day..."

Thousand-Yard Shots All Around

MOONLIGHT RESERVE GOLF CLUB

As Fuentes and A.C. walked into the golf club restaurant, Fuentes stopped and looked around in surprise; the place was empty.

Greg, the director of golf at the Reserve, had seen them out in the parking lot—they'd come over to pick up the car Fuentes had left the day before—and he came over immediately and grasped Fuentes by the shoulder.

"Doc, how you doing?"

"Don't worry about me, Greg. I'll be fine."

"Well, we're all still in a complete state of shock," Greg said. He swept his hand around the room. "And as you can see, everyone's staying away today. Well, except for Jerry Hood."

"Yeah, they don't want to get shot," said a voice behind them.

Fuentes turned and saw that it was Nick. "I can't say I blame them," said Fuentes. "It was hard for me to come back here today; I can tell you that." He turned to A.C., standing beside them. "Nick, Greg, I'd like you to meet my friend, A.C. LaFleur, visiting here from New York. A.C., Greg is the director here; Nick is our head pro."

As the three shook hands, Greg said, "I've heard a lot about you, Mr. LaFleur."

"Same here," added Nick. "You have quite a reputation. We've all heard the stories."

"Well, Michael here tends to exaggerate," A.C. replied.

"Not when it comes to you, A.C.," Fuentes said emphatically. "No exaggeration necessary."

A.C. cocked his head in appreciation. He and Fuentes had been through a lot together, and the respect was mutual.

"Do you have time to talk?" Greg asked. "A lot happened after you left yesterday."

Fuentes nodded in quick agreement. "I was going to ask you the same thing."

As they settled at a table, Nick asked, "Have you talked with the sheriff yet?"

Fuentes shook his head. "No, not at all. I guess he called the house yesterday afternoon, but I hadn't made it home yet."

"Lots of speculation going on," Greg said, as the waitress came over to the table. "Rampant speculation, I'd say."

"Good morning, everyone," the waitress said as she passed out menus.

"Good morning, Sheryl, thanks. We'll just be a few minutes."

"Sure thing."

After they had all taken a look at the menu, A.C. leaned forward. "Rampant speculation, you were saying."

"Right. Well, to be fair, they don't have much to go on. First, he asked for witnesses, but no one had seen a thing. I think that Doc was the only one who saw anything."

"I guess that's right," said Fuentes. "I had just come over the hill when I heard the shot and saw Mike go down. But I didn't see anything else."

"There was a lot of understandable confusion regarding what happened," Nick said. "There wasn't even agreement on what direction the shots came from. Or even how many shots there were."

"There were only two," Fuentes said.

"Yesterday, I heard one guy say four, another three," said Greg. "And that they came from the direction of the Headwaters Grille."

"That's out that direction, A.C.," said Fuentes, pointing back toward Moonlight, "at the base of one of the big ski lifts."

"In any case," Greg went on, "there's been no shooter identified, or even the shooting site. So, no real suspects. Which is not surprising. Who in hell would shoot Mike?"

There was a pause while Sheryl came over and took their orders.

"You said 'real suspects,' Greg," Fuentes said after they had ordered. "What is the sheriff saying? Any plan?"

"He's going to start by looking at anyone with local knowledge and marksmanship skills. Then try to match that up with a motive."

"There are a lot of folks around here with the skills," Nick said. "Even for a long shot, which is the most likely scenario."

Fuentes scratched his head and frowned. "But it had to have been something like a thousand-yard shot, or close to it, based on what I heard on the course yesterday. The sound came from a long way off, from across the valley."

"There are plenty around here who could make a shot like that. Or who claim they can. Anyway, that's where they're starting."

"Are they looking at anyone in particular?"

"Well, I don't want to fan the flames of speculation," Greg said carefully. "I'm just repeating what I heard yesterday."

A.C. pulled a small notebook and a pencil from his pocket. Greg looked alarmed.

"Oh, don't worry," A.C. said, reassuringly. "I'll be discreet. It's an old habit; I have to write everything down."

Mollified, especially given A.C.'s reputation, Greg continued. "The initial focus at the moment is on the Moonlight security team, but I think that's only because they have the requisite shooting skills. As far as opportunity, motive, who knows? Anyway, first there's Matt."

"Head of security," Fuentes told A.C., in a quick aside.

"Right. Matt has been heard to say—often—that he's the best marksman around. Brags that he makes thousand-yard shots routinely. He wasn't on duty yesterday, and says he was down in Big Sky at the time of the shooting. Then there's Chris. Ex-Coast Guard, trained as a sniper, and he's said that he can make a shot far longer than even a thousand. What the Coast Guard needs with snipers, I don't know. In any case, he claims to have been patrolling at the other end of Moonlight when the shooting occurred, but can't prove it. Finally, there's Geno, originally from Wisconsin, a big Packer fan. One of his regular duties is to patrol Jack Creek Road. He says he was at the bottom gate at the time, all the way down by Ennis."

Too Many Suspects Can Ruin a Good Mystery

MOONLIGHT LODGE

"Everyone who worked for Moonlight Security was a suspect?" I asked. "That doesn't say much for the security team."

"Reagan, you have to remember that the sheriff was working completely in the dark at this point. Don't jump to conclusions. I'm getting to that, anyway. A lot of it has to do with the general environment up here. Gun use is not only common, it's practically required."

Nick turned to LaFleur. "I want to emphasize that all three of the security guys have excellent employment records. No hint of trouble at any previous job. All well-liked and respected in the community."

"Good to know," said A.C., making a quick notation in his pad. "In their position I might have focused on them first myself."

"Is anyone else a suspect?" Fuentes asked.

"There are quite a few local hunters, well known in the area. Sam, for one—"

"You can't be serious," Fuentes broke in. "Sam?" Sam was a well-known figure around Moonlight, (Mike Wilcynski's boss, and a close friend), and was deeply involved in both the golf club and the community. An avid skier and sailor, Sam had recently expressed interest in becoming a hunter.

Greg raised his hands in a gesture of *yeah, I know*. "Well, he has really been getting his Western skills together recently, which includes hunting and shooting. And the property up along Jack Creek Road right across from the course is part of his Moonlight holdings. So, that makes him a suspect. They're not ruling out anyone at this point. Of course, there are other, contradictory theories regarding Moonlight, even more far-fetched, in my opinion. This morning in the regular staff meeting we were told that someone in the Boston head office is worried that this could be just the beginning. Sam apparently just turned down a hostile takeover offer, and the conjecture is that this could be the start of terrorist campaign designed to force a short sale. Or something like that." Nick sat by shaking his head.

A.C. looked up from his notepad. "You said the sheriff has some other motives in mind as well?"

"Yeah, but they're all pretty tenuous. Someone unhappy with the way the Reserve is run, maybe, or a disgruntled environmental crusader; someone out to disrupt the rapid development that's going on, same rationale. It was even suggested that with Mike out of the way, Nick and I are potentially next in line for the management job, making both of us suspects."

"Leaving no stone unturned," said Nick, half in disgust. "A lot of people around here are pretty unhappy with the questioning, but I suppose it's necessary."

"Here's lunch," said Greg, as Sheryl brought over their meals. "Thank you, Sheryl. Oh, yeah, Doc, I haven't been able to contact Mike's family. Has that been done?"

"Unfortunately, no. Mike told me the other day that his wife and two daughters are on some sort of eco-expedition in the mountains of Portugal, and will be out of cellphone range for another week."

"Damn. But that reminds me, were you expecting someone to meet you out on the course? I got an odd phone call the day before yesterday. Someone asking about you. Said he was a friend of a friend."

"He didn't say who it was?"

"That's the thing. I asked how he knew you, and he gave me the name of one of the other members, and said he'd been trying to get in touch with you. So, I figured it was okay. I told him you're out on the course every morning, with that crazy hat of yours. That was alright, I hope?"

"Sure, Greg. No problem."

"Oh, and I have your hat in the back room. I didn't know what to do with it, since…well, anyway, do you want it?"

"Um, yeah, I should take it. Thanks."

At that, the conversation turned away from the shooting, as Greg and Nick tried to lighten the mood. A.C. told a long story about the fire-bombing of his houseboat in the marina in Oswego, and the others talked golf and wildlife, which commonly went together on the Reserve course.

Polished Brass

DOC'S HOUSE

"I just don't see how they can suspect anyone from Moonlight," Maggie said. The group was gathered out on the patio with drinks and snacks, being briefed on the conversation that had taken place at the golf club.

"The sheriff seems to be taking a rather scatter-gun approach to all this," said Fuentes. "I thought better of him. I don't understand it."

A.C. reached for some cheese and crackers. "In cases like this, with no weapon, no motive, no witnesses, not even a crime scene, his options are very limited," he counseled. "He's got to sift through a big pile of potential profiles, looking for anything that will point in the right direction. Hoping someone will squeal on an acquaintance, or come forward with seemingly irrelevant information that could tie someone to the crime.

"But I agree with the general consensus that it had to be a long, sniper-style shot. Nothing else fits."

"Absolutely," said Frank. "And it sounds like there's no shortage of potential shooters."

Fuentes leaned forward and topped off his floater. "A good eighty percent of Montana residents consider themselves hunters, and a good percentage of those believe they're capable of making a thousand-yard shot. If pressed, they'll qualify that by conceding it takes the right rifle, ammo, a good scope, and the right conditions. But I suppose you're right, A.C., the sheriff does have a large pool of suspects to wade through." He raised a hand. "Oh, and that reminds me—I checked on Sam, and he's actually away at a sailing competition off the coast of Vietnam."

"That would make it a *very* long shot," said Frank. They ignored him.

Jamila turned to A.C., a querulous look on her face. "You said a minute ago that there's no agreement among the witnesses about where the shot came from; that doesn't make sense to me."

"Oh, that's very common," explained A.C., as he, too, refilled his glass. "There's almost never a good correspondence among witnesses, even for things much more straightforward than just sounds. Witnesses often contradict one another on physical descriptions of a suspect—hair color, clothes, even whether or not there was any facial hair. They almost always miss smaller, distinguishing characteristics. No, I'm not surprised that there were differing accounts of the shots. But I do wonder how you can be sure about what you heard, Doc. How you can be so positive about the direction and sound of the shots."

"That doesn't surprise me," said Maggie. "I worked with Michael long enough to understand how much he always relied on sounds in the operating room to judge what was going on with his patient. He's like you, in a way, A.C., sort of old-school at times." Fuentes smiled at the complimentary comparison. "He was never a big fan of all the digital monitors they use these days. Even if they had audible signals, he felt they were too generic, easily becoming just part of the background noise.

"So, he used all kinds of tricks to help him monitor the patient directly. Sometimes, he even placed a small whistle in the patient's mouth in just the right way so that the sound would change if something was wrong," she said, turning to Fuentes. He nodded in agreement. "And other things, too," she went on, "I can't remember them all. But anyway, if Michael says the two gunshot sounds were different, and that they came from across the valley, then I believe him."

"It appears to me," said A.C., reflectively, "that we are not all that happy with the way the sheriff's investigation is going, no slight intended. Is there something we can do to help?"

"Are you sure you want to get involved? You're on vacation!"

Frank stood up. "Got a topo map, Doc? A.C., let's go take a look, this time in the right direction."

I surveyed the Moonlight bar as Fuentes absented himself momentarily to greet someone coming in. The room was getting very crowded, and a little noisy. It suddenly got even noisier as a large group entered and boisterously arranged themselves along the bar in the area that Fuentes had named "Mahogany Ridge," calling out to friends and greeting the bartender with gusto.

"Who's that, Ethan?" I asked.

"Ah! The James Gang has just arrived in Moonlight."

"James Gang? As in Jesse James?"

"That's right. They like to think they are carrying on one of the oldest and most revered traditions of the West—carrying on!" said Ethan, laughing. "I'll definitely have to reorder my high-end bourbon and Scotch after they depart next week."

"I'm starting to learn that the terms 'normal' and 'Moonlight' seldom occupy the same sentence."

"You're catching on; and that key understanding is what could make this article of yours a Pulitzer Prize winner!"

Fuentes returned and sat down. I leaned towards him and spoke up to make myself heard. "We were talking about gun use," I said. "The gun culture in Montana is pretty unique for this country, I think. Well, here and Wyoming, Idaho, maybe the Dakotas. I guess it makes sense that there were a lot of suspects. You're right, people up here take their guns seriously."

"And yet, for all that, gun violence is much lower here than in many other places," said Fuentes. "As widespread as gun ownership is, you'd think otherwise."

"I had quite an experience at a trial recently," I said. "It was a gun-related case—an out-of-stater brandished a gun at a man and his wife and kid during a minor road rage incident. I was reporting on the case and was in court for the jury selection. The lawyers had quite a time of it; when they asked—as they had to in this case— who in the jury selection pool owned a gun, everyone's hand came up, all thirty of them. Then one of the lawyers asked, okay, who has a gun with them today? All thirty hands went up again – men, women, old ladies, the whole group."

"You see what the sheriff was up against."

"Yeah. Alright, so you went out looking for the shooting site. What did you find?"

"Frank and A.C. went out; they had the most expertise when it came to things like this."

"You've mentioned Frank only very briefly, when we first met. Why would he be the one to go with A.C.? A.C. was a detective, so it's natural he would be good at this, but what's Frank's background? You said he was a chef, but also that he had quite an interesting history."

"Ah, well. I could write a book. But here's the short version. He was called 'Big Frank' for a reason, six feet tall and over two hundred pounds, solid but agile. After leaving the military, he went into government service—an unnamed agency. I always assumed NSA, but A.C. said no, probably CIA. Or the other way around, maybe. In any case, he was very experienced in all types of surveillance and related operations. A lot of black ops, we suspected. Crazy skills. And along with that, possible PTSD. LaFleur met him at a veteran's benefit; Frank was at loose ends at the time, they hit it off, and soon Frank became almost part of the family. He kept himself off meds through his friendship with the group, and the socialization he got working as the chef at the 1850 House. He's been in on several of the cold cases A.C. has gotten himself involved in from time to time."

"Which brings us back to A.C., and your past experiences. You've hinted about working 'cold cases' together, but what does that mean, exactly? How did you two get together again?"

"It was in, oh, 2006 or so, when Maggie—it was Maggie Malone, then—finagled A.C. and me into working on a murder case together, something that had happened at the hospital forty years earlier. Well, we didn't know at the time that it was murder, it had been declared a suicide under very unusual circumstances; but anyway, that's how we got together. Since then, there have been three more cases, each one with its own challenges. Then things settled down, and a few years ago A.C. bought the 1850 House you've heard me mention; eventually he and Maggie got married."

"I'm intrigued. You'll have to tell me the full stories someday."

"Someday. For now, let's concentrate on Elk Knob."

ELK KNOB, JACK CREEK ROAD

They drove along the upper section of Jack Creek Road that lay directly opposite the golf course, stopping and getting out periodically to reconnoiter. The seventeenth hole was visible from several points along the road.

"Looks like a helluva long ways down there, Frank," commented A.C. at the first stop.

"Not for someone who knows what they're doing," he answered. "Oh, no way could I make a shot like that. But there are plenty who can."

"And one who did."

"No joke."

It was about ten minutes later that they spotted an old green pickup truck parked on a short spur, a short way off of the road. They pulled over and parked just above it, well off on the shoulder.

"Local vehicle," LaFleur commented, noting the Montana plates and a "Catch It All in Ennis" bumper sticker. "Hasn't been here all that long, by the look of it." They got out of the car and surveyed the road, looking for anything out of the ordinary.

"I'll look around a bit," said Frank. He walked back in the direction of Moonlight about fifty yards while LaFleur examined the truck, already making notes.

"Nothing more in that direction," Frank said as he returned to the pickup. "What about the truck?"

"Doors are locked, nothing visible inside. Gun rack is empty. The engine appears to be cold, but it's hard to say how long it's been here. Not a lot of dust on it. So, maybe here a couple of days, or maybe just a couple of hours."

"That means there could be someone else out here right now, doing the same thing we're doing. Looking for the shooting site."

A.C. furrowed his brows. "Or setting up for another seventeenth-hole sniping session."

Frank started. "That's a chilling thought."

"Okay, then," LaFleur said, looking around a little more apprehensively than before, "with that in mind, let's see what we can find." He slipped his notebook into this pocket. "Let's start right here, then go a bit farther down the road if we don't find anything," he said, motioning towards Ennis.

They moved off of the road and began to make their way down a gently sloping hill. Small open areas, covered with meadow grass and dotted with small white wildflowers, were interspersed among thick clusters of small, dark green fir trees. The golf course was intermittently visible in the background between the trees, looking much farther away than it actually was. Fan Mountain loomed grandly in the distance behind the course, a gray scarp blanketed at the base by a soft spread of green.

A.C. and Frank had to intentionally tear their attention away from the spectacular scenery to focus on the task ahead, all the while reminding themselves of the possibility that they may not be alone out there. Picking their way down the slope on the soft ground, stepping over the occasional dead log, they initiated a sweep search of the terrain in front of and below them, automatically keeping an optimal distance of about twenty-five yards between them—far enough apart to facilitate good coverage, but still close enough to allow good communication.

"Anything?" Frank called, quietly.

"Nope."

"Let's move a bit to the south."

"That's to the left?"

"Right. Um, correct," Frank clarified, then waved downslope, to an open area just below and to the left of where LaFleur had stopped.

"Right. I mean, okay." LaFleur waited a moment for Frank to come down the hill. As soon as Frank was in position, they started out together.

They were only about fifty yards farther down the hill when A.C. suddenly stopped and held his arms up in the air.

"Hold it!" he said urgently, quickly motioning for Frank to join him.

"I see it," Frank said a moment later, as A.C. pointed down the hill. "Looks like a perfect spot."

About thirty yards below them, just past a low group of juniper bushes, they saw a short shooting tripod set up on the edge of a clear, level area that extended just past the junipers. Beyond that, the Moonlight Reserve golf course stretched out far below them, towards Lone Peak, the concrete cart path running like a bright, white river through the alternating light and dark green of the fairways, roughs, and greens and the brownish scrub of the native areas.

As they edged closer to the clearing, side by side, Frank pointed out something glinting in the afternoon sun, bright and brassy, on the ground out near the tripod.

"Cartridge?"

"Could be."

"Looks like we found the shooting site."

"I'd say so. Let's hope there's some good evidence."

A.C. led the way down the hill with Frank still at his side, both moving cautiously, eyeing the surrounding area as they went. As they rounded the junipers, what they found stopped them both in their tracks.

"Oh, my God," uttered LaFleur. He reached up and pulled off his cap, ran his hand through his thick gray hair, replaced the cap, and then in a calmer voice said, "I sure as hell wasn't expecting *this*."

Letting out a deep breath, Frank silently agreed, simply turning to LaFleur and nodding.

Sprawled on its back next to the thick bushes was the body of a short, middle-aged, stocky man. He was dressed in faded camo and old leather boots, legs sticking out at an unnatural angle. A rifle and a handgun lay on the ground next to him. There was an obvious entry wound in the left side of the man's forehead, which was splotchy purple and white, as was the rest of his face. His thick, graying hair was blotted with black, dried blood.

"Perfect spot," repeated Frank, as they both stood next to the body. "Seventeenth hole right down there. You can even see the pin from here, plain as day."

"I'll call Doc," said A.C., pulling out his phone. "We'll need the local sheriff out here."

"Hold on a minute," said Frank. "Let's take a closer look before we get a crowd milling around."

A.C. grunted, either in self-disgust or approval, it wasn't clear. "I'm really getting out of practice," was all he said. "Yeah, you're right, let's try to find out what we can while we have the chance."

A.C. bent down closer to the body and got a strong, acrid whiff of putrefaction—something he'd hoped never to encounter again after he left the force. The hole in the man's head had already been colonized by blowflies—he could make out tiny maggots wriggling in the recesses of the wound. He carefully placed the side of his hand on the bare skin of the man's arm.

"Cold." He nudged the arm and it moved, but very slightly. "Still some rigor mortis," he said, "so that means he's probably been dead less than thirty-six hours. Face looks somewhat relaxed, as well, so rigor may be fading. Weather's been fairly warm, so it's hard to tell exactly."

"Well, Mike was shot at about seven in the morning, day before yesterday, so that's, what, thirty-four—no, thirty-two hours."

"Right. Fits in exactly with the condition of the body. But there's something here I really don't get," said A.C, as he stood up. "If he's the shooter—"

"—then why is he dead with a bullet in his head?" finished Frank. "Yeah."

"Let's take a look around. Maybe there's something else going on here, but it's sure as hell not obvious," said Frank, moving carefully down the hill, stopping a few feet below the body. "Careful as you move around, A.C.," he said, over his shoulder. "I think I can make out some tracks leading in and out, there to the left."

"I see them," confirmed A.C., as he came up behind Frank. They both stood quietly for a minute or so, each processing the scene in his own way. Frank concentrated on the physical details—the position of the two firearms lying on the ground near the body, the handgun and rifle; a spent cartridge on the ground close by; a tripod set up near his feet; the style, color, and disarray of the man's clothing. And the short-range gunshot to the head, clearly visible even from a few feet away.

A.C., while acutely aware of the same details after the quick forensic examination he'd made, was now thinking more in terms of actions, that is, the sequence of events that could have led to the configuration they saw before them—the approach, the setup, the execution of the shot, the aftermath—ending up with the unlikely circumstance of the shooter lying dead beside his rifle. He always tried to gain an impression of the overall "attitude" of a crime scene before diving to deeply into the details. It was one of his idiosyncrasies, and had gained him a reputation as an oddball on the force in the old days. But results mattered, and he had always had the best record in the department.

So, each coming from a different perspective, and each thinking exactly the same thing: *What the hell had gone on here?*

"The handgun looks like a Smith & Wesson," said Frank, gesturing. "Not a .500, though, probably not even a .44. Looks like a .357."

A.C. bent down and took a close look. "You're right. I suppose they carry them here for bear protection?"

"According to Doc, a .357 isn't big enough, and anyway, bear spray is much better. You know the old joke, shooting a bear just makes him mad."

Frank edged over closer to the body, on the opposite side of the hill from the tracks they had seen. He bent down and looked around for a second, then picked up a small twig. Carefully slipping it into the open end of the shell casing, he held it up to the light. A.C. moved closer, leaning over to take a look.

"It's been polished," Frank said.

A.C. nodded, and Frank placed it back on the ground where he'd found it. They both stood up, and A.C. stepped back while Frank took several pictures.

"I'd better give Doc a call now," said A.C., reaching again for his phone.

"Right."

After briefly telling Fuentes of their discovery, A.C. turned to Frank. "He'll call Moonlight security and the sheriff."

"Okay, good." Frank moved gingerly—surprisingly so for such a big man—to where he'd pointed out the tracks. He stared intently at an indistinct path of lightly crushed grass for a few moments, then took a closer look at a few footprints in a small patch of soft soil. Pulling out his phone, he took several more pictures. He shifted higher up the hill, to another large patch of open dirt, peering down at the ground for a long minute. "Something funny about those tracks," he said, as he came back to where A.C. was standing.

"What's that?"

"I'd say that two people came in, but only one went out," he said. "And it obviously wasn't our friend, here."

"That puts a different complexion on things."

"Yes, doesn't it?"

"There's something odd about the head wound, as well," said A.C., who had been thoughtfully reviewing possible scenarios while Frank studied the tracks. "Can't quite put my finger on it, but something's not right. Would love to be there at the post-mortem."

Frank pointed down at the rifle lying on the ground. "Interesting rifle, don't you think, A.C.? And not exactly what I would call a hunting rifle, if I don't miss my guess."

"Oh, c'mon, Frank, I know you, and you very seldom guess."

"Okay, then. Dragonov SVD. With a top scope." Frank suddenly looked up the hill. "Someone's coming."

They both quickly stepped away from the body, went back up the hill twenty yards or so, then turned and waited. A tall man in a black uniform soon came into view from behind some small trees and walked quickly up to them.

"Geno, Moonlight Security," he said, as he approached. "Michael Fuentes called in a report of an, um, incident?"

"Glad to see you," replied A.C, putting out his hand. "A.C. LaFleur." Geno shook his hand briefly and turned to Frank.

"Frank Ivanovich," said Frank, reaching for Geno's hand. "Thanks for coming so quickly."

"No problem. I was close by. Jack Creek's my territory." He looked past the two men and spotted the body. "Jesus."

It was another twenty or thirty minutes before they heard a vehicle pull up and stop on the road. While they'd been waiting, Geno had taken quite a few pictures, but there had been little talk of the crime, and they'd finally all moved back upslope about twenty feet, away from the body.

"Hey, Geno!" someone called out a couple of minutes later.

"Hello, Deputy," Geno answered, as a small, dark-haired woman in a trim, tan uniform came down the hill towards them.

"What've we got?" the woman asked as soon as she got to them.

"Hard to say," Geno answered, "other than we've got a dead body on the side of the hill. Just over there," he said, motioning to the juniper bushes just below them.

"Okay, let's take a look." She started in that direction, then stopped and looked over at A.C. and Frank. "You the two gentlemen who found it?"

"Yes," they answered together.

"Touch anything?"

"Nope." "No, ma'am."

"Sarah, this is Frank Ivanovich," pointing to Frank, "and A.C. LaFleur. Guests of Dr. Fuentes from Moonlight."

"How'd you two happen to be up here?" she asked.

"Well, this might sound a little irresponsible," said A.C., improvising quickly, "but we were over here looking for bears. We've heard so many stories about bears wandering around, but haven't seen one since we've been here, and Doc thought this might be a good place to spot one. More out in the open, he said, and close to the road. He thought that would be safer than coming across one on a narrow trail."

"Hmmm. I suppose so. Got your bear spray?"

"Uh, back in the car," Frank answered, looking a bit sheepish.

Sarah gave him a return look, as if to say, *well, won't do you much good there, will it?* but just said "Okay," then continued down the hill, with Geno following. A.C. and Frank stayed slightly behind.

"Just up ahead there," said Geno.

As Sarah came around to the front of the junipers and saw the body, she stopped and gave a loud gasp. "Oh, my God. Shorty!" she exclaimed. "What in—"

"You know him?" Geno asked. "Who is he?"

"Shorty Dalles. Works at Shedhorn Sports, down in Ennis. He's been a fixture there for years. Hunting, guiding, firearms specialist; he's been there for as long as I can remember. I should have recognized the truck." She looked around. "What was he *doing* up here?"

She bent down and looked at the wound in Shorty's head, murmuring to herself in low tones. Then she made her way carefully around the area, stooping occasionally to look at something more closely, basically repeating what Frank and A.C. had already done before she and Geno had arrived.

"Geno, ever seen a rifle like that?"

"Nope. Looks like something out of Star Wars. I'll bet you could see the rings of Saturn with that scope."

"Or the seventeenth hole at Moonlight."

"Yes, there's that."

"Could be something exotic Shedhorn has going for their wealthier clientele." She went back to her examination.

After a few minutes, she walked back over to where the rest of them were standing, stopped, stretched her shoulders back, and said, "Right."

"What now, Sarah?" asked Geno.

"First thing, I'll notify the Madison County sheriff's office; they can contact his wife. Then we'll take care of things here." She shook her head. "Damn. Well, I guess I'm not that surprised."

"Not surprised? What do you mean?" asked Geno. LaFleur and Frank looked at one another, then back at the deputy, both obviously wondering the same thing.

"Well, maybe that's not the best way to put it. Not surprised that he did something crazy, I mean. And not surprised he killed himself." She looked around, still shaking her head slowly. "But why in hell did he think it was necessary to take somebody else with him?" She sighed. "Oh, yeah, old Shorty's been messed up for a long time now. I've got a friend on the force in Ennis, she told me they've been having a hell of a time with him down there. His wife moved out of the house, since he was getting so violent; she even had to have a restraining order filed against him. And he'd been banned from the Gravel Bar after an incident there a few weeks ago. Fired his pistol into the ceiling during a fight. Could've killed someone."

"Why wasn't he locked up?" asked LaFleur.

"He did spend a couple of days in jail. I don't know when he was set for trial."

"But still, why would he do something like this?" asked Geno.

"I guess he finally just went over the edge," she said. "His family tried several times to get him into a mental health program in Bozeman, after a couple of, well, scary psychotic episodes, I guess you'd call them. He began showing definite signs of being—you know, 'a danger to himself and others.' He was barely able to hold on to his job at Shedhorn. I think they kept him on the payroll just trying to keep him occupied, hoping he'd be able get professional help."

"Couldn't the county do anything?" asked LaFleur.

"Madison County doesn't have a lot of mental health resources. Ennis even less. They were doing the best they could."

LaFleur and Frank made themselves inconspicuous while watching the deputy survey the scene, standing a bit off to the side and conversing in low tones. As far as they could tell, the deputy had noticed nothing unusual about the shell casing—she'd just placed it in an evidence bag without looking at it closely. Frank also didn't think she'd seen the other set of tracks leading away from the site, the tracks that he believed showed a second person had been involved.

While she was gathering up evidence and marking the site, an ambulance had arrived. By the time the EMTs had removed the body, the area had been well trampled.

"Good thing we got here first," Frank said. A.C. nodded in agreement.

I set my glass down on the bar. "So, it was murder/suicide. Pretty clear cut."

"It sure seemed like it," replied Fuentes. "The deputy, Sarah Upfield, knew Shorty's history. And here he was, alone on a mountainside in a remote part of the county, with a revolver lying next to his body and a gunshot wound to the head. And she was aware of the results of the initial investigation of the shooting the day before at the club, that is, that no one had a clue as to who shot Mike, or why. Now she knew who, but why? Well, who knows what goes on in someone's mind when in that state?"

"Did the investigation go any farther than that? What was the official response from the department, once she reported in? Wouldn't they have launched an investigation?"

"They didn't have time. Once they'd examined the scene and moved the body to the morgue, everything was put on ice—excuse the pun—at least until the more immediate crisis, the wildfires, was under control.

"We talked with the sheriff's department late that afternoon, as soon as Frank and A.C. got back from Elk Knob. We talked to the sheriff directly, in fact, and he confirmed what the deputy had told them at the scene. For the time being, as far as the department was concerned, Shorty had some bizarre reason for what he had done, now known only to himself and God. He'd simply gone crazy, shot Mike, maybe as the first victim in a random series of shootings. Then before going any farther with it, he collapsed in remorse and shot himself. That's how a lot of shootings like this end, after all."

"Yeah, that's true."

The Ugly Hat

DOC'S HOUSE

Dinner had been surprisingly relaxed considering the events of the past two days. A.C. and Frank had given everyone an overview of what had taken place on Elk Knob earlier that afternoon, of course, but it had been agreed to put it all aside for a while, in order to decompress a bit. Now they were all gathered at the bar downstairs.

A.C. led off the conversation. "Mike was shot because of a double switch."

"What?"

"What switch?"

"What do you mean?"

"All in due time. But first let's lay out what we know to be true," he went on. "We're looking for an explanation that fits all the facts, notwithstanding the sheriff's theory of murder-slash-suicide, which I have come to strongly doubt. I'm not going to use the standard profiling technique here, but something you've all heard me talk about many times, the logical principle called Ockham's Razor."

"Excuse me?" I interrupted. "Something 'razor?' What is he talking about?"

"It's a principle, or logical technique, really," explained Fuentes. "Ockham's razor, named after a fourteenth century philosopher, William of Ockham. It's one of A.C.'s standard practices. The common version is that the simplest explanation that fits all of the facts, no matter how improbable, is more than likely the right one. More correctly, it states that when choosing between more than one possible explanation, choose the one that makes the fewest assumptions. The Latin source from a work by Ockham is usually translated as "It is futile to do with more things that which can be done with fewer."

"That sounds like a useful tool for a detective."

"It's what makes A.C. one of the best."

"Okay, sorry, please go on."

"First," said LaFleur, "there's the evidence from the crime scene that Frank described. Paramount is his observation that the shell casing was polished. That, and the type of rifle used. These were the unmistakable marks of a professional."

"What do you mean, A.C.?" asked Jamila. "That Shorty was a professional hunter?"

"Not that kind of professional. But let me finish, there's more— the shell casing just started me down what I believe is the right road. Frank also looked very closely at tracks coming in and out of the area. He's sure that Shorty did not hike down there alone. On top of that, the tracks of the second individual were peculiar. Frank, care to elaborate?"

Frank leaned forward, holding up his phone to display the photos he'd taken. "I wasn't sure until I was able to take a close look at the pictures I took. But now I'm certain of it. The second person's tracks exhibit some type of disability—a pronounced limp, some deformity, perhaps even a prosthetic limb."

"How could you tell all that from just looking at footprints in the grass?" Jamila sounded skeptical.

Frank shrugged. "To quote Sherlock Holmes: 'Happily, I have laid great stress upon it, and much practice has made it second nature to me.'" He smiled. "Go on, please, A.C.," he said.

"Okay. Just as an aside, there's another thing that has been nagging at me. At lunch, Greg mentioned that he'd received a phone call a couple of days ago—from someone who didn't identify themselves—asking for Doc. Could that have been this second person? It's very suspicious, in any case. So, regarding that, we've enlisted a local computer guru—a friend of Doc's named F.T. O'Connor—who says he can set up a program to monitor the CCTV footage in and out of the Jack Creek Road gates. Some sort of AI 'bot,' he called it. That should keep us on top of things.

"Okay, where were we…polished casing, Shorty wasn't alone…then third, the gunshot wound to Shorty's head. Frank and I agree that it did not look self-inflicted."

"But if that were obvious, wouldn't the coroner figure that out?" Maggie asked.

"Sure, and he certainly will, when he gets around to it. But that doesn't help us right now. Also," he continued, "don't forget Doc's earlier description of the shots he heard. Based on that, we can trust the fact that there were only two shots fired—a pistol shot first, followed not long after by one shot from a high-powered rifle."

A.C. looked over at Fuentes. "That brings me to you, Doc. When we went to pick up your car yesterday, Doc, I saw the hat Greg brought out to you. He was carrying it rather gingerly, and I couldn't help but notice it was covered in blood. It struck me as rather odd. Oh, it's an odd hat in itself – those colors! But why, I thought to myself, was *your* hat covered with blood?" He looked pointedly at Fuentes, behind the bar. "Greg had called it 'your hat' a couple of times, so it was, plainly, your hat." He turned back to the group. "Like I said, it seemed odd at the time, and at first, I thought, well, it must have gotten that way accidentally, while Doc was tending to Mike before the ambulance got there. From what we heard, there was a *lot* of blood. And Doc was trying his best to save Mike's life with nothing but a golf towel.

"But then it came to me." He paused, with another hard look at Fuentes. "Doc, why was your hat so bloody?"

Fuentes stopped in the middle of pouring his floater, staring at LaFleur. "I had switched hats with Mike that morning, before he got there. As a joke."

"He'd switched hats," A.C. repeated. "Which means that Mike was shot—by someone—for wearing the wrong hat." He paused a moment to let this sink in. "It's no coincidence that Mike was shot immediately after you brought home the wrong bag, Doc," he continued. "Now that I know for sure about the hat, it's clear. Mike was not the target, Doc, you were."

Fuentes just sat there quietly, but Maggie exclaimed at this. "A.C., this is crazy! You are always finding connections, and I have to admit that you are almost always right, but this time? I can't believe it."

Jamila also registered her concern. "But there's no reason anyone would want to kill Michael, any more than they would want to kill Mike Wilcynski!"

"No, Jamila, it all fits. And it's all tied to the Macdonald woman at the airport. The clincher is the carry-ons; Ms. Macdonald's bag, with the Pappy Van Winkle in it, and Doc's bag, which went missing at the airport. Whoever has that bag now knows who Doc is, where he lives. And that 'whoever' is a murderer. A clever one, at that, to judge by the quick response. And there's not just one of them—Doc said he saw two men following Ms. Macdonald at the airport. They've very quickly worked up a profile of our good friend here, know his comings and goings, even that he wears an ugly pink and yellow ball cap on the golf course. It was a case of mistaken identity that got Mike shot, nothing more. First the bag, then the hat. A double switch."

"Now what, A.C.?" asked Fuentes. "What's our next move?"

"To start with," A.C. answered, "I want to grill Ethan about Pappy Van Winkle; he can surely provide some insight into how to determine whether in fact what we have is counterfeit. That has to be the key to understanding what Ms. Macdonald was doing out here. Why was she carrying counterfeit whiskey—and an unlabeled, empty bottle—and if that is in fact what it turns out to be, how did that get her killed?

"I want to try to track her movements all the way up until the time she got to the airport. Unless we determine exactly what she was up to, we can't defend ourselves. I want to narrow down the possibilities, at least."

"Well, that's what you're good at, A.C.; wheat from the chaff, and all that."

"Well, we're starting with a lot of chaff, that's for sure. One other thing, Doc—we can't let them know you're alive. You need to lay low. I'm even worried about the trip out to the golf club today, but that couldn't be helped, and besides, we didn't know then what we know now. Let's see, have you used your phone since the shooting?"

"No, I don't think I've even touched it. There's been too much going on."

"Good. Let's avoid any communication using your phone until we know more. It appears that we are dealing with a very talented, not to mention ruthless, gang here, and they are obviously on a short schedule."

"So, we should run," interjected Jamila. "Get the hell out of here."

"No, I don't think so, Jamila," A.C. replied. "They know too much about Doc, maybe about everyone here. Our only advantage, and I really hate to say this, is that they apparently think they've shot—and killed—Doc. That gives us an edge, since they are probably moving on now to whatever it was that brought them here after the Macdonald woman." He paused. "No, we can't run from this. They're sure to follow. We're going to have to stay here and deal with this, here and now.

"And we don't have any time to waste."

I swirled the last drops of Grouse around, listening to the wet swish of small bits of ice circling in the bottom of the glass.

"So, you were the target all along," I said to Fuentes. "Wow."

"Yeah."

"But, Doc—*why*? Why shoot anyone? Mike, or you? What was the motive?"

"Well, it's not at all straightforward. That's not where it ended. And don't worry, I'll get to that."

"Sorry. I'm just getting so wrapped up in it. I can't wait to find out what happens next. I just hope I can do the story justice." I paused and refocused. "Okay, back to our mystery killer. What did A.C. do next? You said he was an investigator back in New York—"

"Police detective."

"Right, and you said a very good one. And that he'd stayed very active after retiring, working on several cold cases."

"And one not so cold, yes. He's very good at what he does."

"I want to know everything—how he thinks, his investigative techniques, how he solved this, step-by-step. Everything."

"Well," Fuentes said thoughtfully, "in that case I guess you should talk directly with him."

PART TWO

The 1850 House

OSWEGO, NEW YORK

"How did your editor decide to send you clear out here?" LaFleur asked. "The paper is a pretty small operation, isn't it? I mean no disrespect; Doc tells me it's quite an important part of the community out there. But still..."

I smiled. "The paper has grown a lot in the ten years since the murders. My editor thinks there is really something to this; it could be the biggest story in the county this year, or for the last ten years, for that matter. And now we have the resources to do it right."

We were sitting at a small table in the bar of the 1850 House. There was a Wurlitzer bubble jukebox on one wall, with a picture of rows of World War II fighter planes above it. There were a few other interesting objects placed in prominent locations around the room, including one of the most enchanting bronzes I had ever seen—the figure of an ice skater caught in mid-pirouette. I made a note to ask LaFleur about it later.

The restaurant/bar had been a fixture in Oswego for many years before LaFleur had purchased it several years before, he explained. He had maintained the eclectic character of the place, keeping it just the way the long time original owner, Joe, had created it, a combination Italian restaurant and flea market—the walls and shelves surrounding the dining room, and the hallway leading to the back bar, were crowded with all sorts of antiques and collectables, all for sale. Over the past two or three years, the stock had been depleted quite a bit, and LaFleur had nearly cleared out the storage room behind the building, and was no longer replenishing items on display.

"I'm very glad you could make it," LaFleur said. "Michael very much wanted me to talk to you. He thought it would be much better for you to get the story first hand."

"Well, I can't thank you enough for taking the time to talk with me."

"Oh, I don't mind at all. Maggie and I have slowed down considerably in the past two years. We don't keep the place open for regular business anymore, we just do special events—wedding receptions, graduation parties, that sort of thing. That keeps us more than busy enough."

"Yes, Doc had mentioned that. Still, I appreciate it."

"Before we get started on my story, I have a question for *you*," LaFleur said. "You seem to be taking this more seriously than just another story. What interests you so much about it?"

"I'm not really sure I can define it. There was something about Doc's story about the encounter in the bar at the airport that I can't get out of my mind. It was just a brief meeting, but one thing I remember in particular—they'd only just met, but she said something like 'I can't wait to see my daughter again.' And a few minutes later, she was murdered. She was my age. And even though I don't know anything about her, I just feel there's a connection somehow. I told you I couldn't really explain it very well."

"Well, you're going to learn a lot more about her this afternoon. And even after ten years, a lot of it still seems like it happened only yesterday. But there's one piece of advice I have for you before we get too far into it. When it comes to this kind of thing," he said, raising a finger to emphasize the point, "don't fall in love with the victim."

He turned his finger around, pointing at himself. "I might have."

How Much Did You Say?

"Ethan, I've got a question for you." LaFleur was sitting at Poet's Corner at the bar. He tried to mask the sense of urgency in his voice. "What do you know about Pappy Van Winkle whiskey?"

"Pappy?" He shot LaFleur a look. "Are you on an expense account?"

"Yeah, pretty expensive stuff, I know. Um, do you have any on hand?"

"Got some right here," Ethan said, turning to the rows of bottles on the shelf behind the bar. He picked one up and set it down on the bar in front of LaFleur. "Here's the top of the line. Family Reserve, 23 Year Old."

LaFleur tilted the bottle back and studied the label. "How much for a shot?"

"Two-hundred and fifty."

LaFleur started counting on his fingers. "Two-fifty times, what, sixteen, eighteen shots to a bottle? Forty-five hundred dollars. Pretty good. Sell a lot?"

"This one? Rarely. The other, lower-priced variety, the Rip Van Winkle, it varies. Quite a bit around holidays, or to a big group celebrating something. It's only fifty bucks a shot."

"Hmm. Would the guys in here who buy it know the difference between Pappy and, say, Jim Beam?"

Ethan smiled. "Probably not. Beam is actually not all that bad, for what it is."

LaFleur set the bottle back upright on the bar. "Would you know how to tell fake from real Pappy?"

Ethan put on a puzzled face, unsure where the conversation was going. "Sure."

"What did you pay for this bottle, by the way?" LaFleur asked.

"Hmmm. Not sure I should say."

"Five hundred?" Ethan made no reply. "I wouldn't know what the price might be, since I sure don't buy it for my bar back home. Not even the lower priced version. Maybe I should." He tapped the side of the bottle with a fingernail. "So, how do you know yours isn't fake?"

"I brought it back directly from the distillery. Went on a junket a year ago."

LaFleur pulled a flask out of the inside pocket of his sport coat. "Try this."

"What is it?"

"Family Reserve, the twenty-three-year old."

"You're kidding."

"Nope. The bottle's sitting over on the bar at Doc's."

"Now I know you're kidding."

"Just give it a try for me."

Ethan poured a small measure into a shot glass and took a sip.

"Nope, not Pappy. Not the Family Reserve. Maybe not even a Pappy at all. Not too bad, but not Pappy."

"You're sure?"

"Yes."

"Can I try a shot of the real stuff?"

"Like I said, are you on an expense account?"

"Charge it to the Doc."

Ethan laughed. "Don't tell anyone I gave you a free shot of Pappy."

"It's our secret."

Ethan pulled out a shot glass and poured a very small dollop. "Just enough to taste," he said. He put another shot glass on the bar. "For your so-called Pappy," he said. LaFleur poured an equally small measure from the flask into that glass, then held both up to the light.

"Looks right," said Ethan, referring to LaFleur's sample. "How do they taste?"

LaFleur took a careful sip from Ethan's genuine Pappy. In the meantime, Ethan had filled a small water glass and placed it on the bar. LaFleur took a small sip of water, then tasted the whiskey from his flask.

"You're absolutely sure yours is genuine?" he asked again. Before Ethan could answer, LaFleur held up a hand. "No, sorry, I trust you."

LaFleur picked up the first glass and drained it. "There's a definite difference," he admitted. "The real thing has a much better

66

finish, much more complex. But I have to tell you, I wouldn't pay two hundred and fifty dollars for it!"

"I'll admit that I don't care for it much myself," said Ethan, chuckling, "but I don't like bourbon in general." He put the bottle of Pappy back behind the bar. "What next?"

LaFleur gazed down at the two empty shot glasses. "I'm not sure. Who else should I talk to about this?"

Ethan hesitated. "Tell me, why is this so important?"

LaFleur hesitated in return. "I'd rather not go into it, at least, not right now. I need to know more about what I'm looking at here. But it is important. It's the only place I have to start."

"Start what? Okay, never mind. Let's see," he continued, "there's Lat down at McAllister's. I know he stocks it for the fly fisherman, the wealthier clientele, anyway. Um, the Bale of Hay in Virginia City might keep some of the regular Pappy for the tourist trade, they get quite a bit of traffic—their claim to fame is being one of the oldest bars in Montana. The Gravel Bar in Ennis, of course. Oh, and there's a place out north on 287, Chick's. Lots of local activity, not sure about high end stuff, though I've heard there are some high stakes poker games on occasion. Friday nights, I think."

"Poker! Now there's something I know a bit about!"

"I've heard of your games back in New York. I guess Doc was a regular?"

"Right. Well, that may give me an opening; always better to have a reason to be somewhere, rather than just wander in off the street. Thanks for the leads." He replaced the flask in his coat pocket and shifted off of his stool. "Oh, no mention of this to anyone."

"Of course."

As LaFleur left the bar, Ethan called out to him. "Detective!" LaFleur turned around. "I forgot to mention one of the best bars in Madison County," he said. "The Pony!"

"Okay, where is it?"

"Easiest one of all to find. It's in Pony, Montana, a little town at the end of the road. Take 283 west out of Harrison."

LaFleur gave him a virtual tip of the hat. "Thanks for everything. I'm sure we'll need to talk again soon."

The McAllister Inn

MCALLISTER, MONTANA

LaFleur sat down at the massive single slab of shellacked pine that made up the bar at the McAllister Inn and introduced himself. After mentioning Ethan's name, Latimer, manager of the bar and restaurant, reached out and shook LaFleur's hand, welcoming him with a friendly, "Call me Lat. How's Ethan? Haven't seen him in a while"

"Ethan's good. I just left him about an hour ago."

"Well, what can I do for you?"

"I'm on sort of a quest," LaFleur explained. "Tracking down Pappy Van Winkle."

"You aren't the first. There's been a real mystique built up around that stuff. Not sure why."

LaFleur looked over Lat's shoulder to the array of bottles on the shelves behind the bar. "I don't see any here."

"Oh, I've got it." Lat reached behind the bottom row of bottles and pulled one out. "By special request only. Don't need to display it. Have to conserve my supply, anyway."

Lat handed the bottle to LaFleur. He held it up to the light, reading the label. "Family Reserve, 23-Year-Old. That's the rare one, isn't it?"

"Yep, hen's teeth, for sure. I was told only six bottles had been brought into all of Montana."

"Wow. What do you have to pay for something like this?"

"Well, the standard gray-market price for the high-end Pappy can go as high as three thousand. I didn't pay anywhere near that."

"Why not?"

"A wholesaler I know owed me a favor. Over the years, I've—well, the details aren't important. In any case, I was able to get this bottle at a very good price."

"What do you get for a single shot?"

"Two twenty-five."

"What if I wanted a Pappy but didn't want to shell out that much? Do you have any other options?"

"Sure." Lat brought out another bottle. "This one's very popular, and not at all hard to get. What you'd call your 'entry level' Pappy, Rip Van Winkle, 107 proof. Retails at about sixty dollars; my price is less, of course."

"What's a shot of that go for?"

"Fifty."

LaFleur shook his head in surprise. "I'm really going to have to consider stocking Pappy at my place."

"Oh, you run a gin joint, do you?"

LaFleur laughed. "Used to. Just do special events now, weddings, bar mitzvahs, you know."

"Sounds better than the daily grind," Lat replied.

LaFleur, reached into his coat pocket. "Say, Lat, could you do me a favor?" Lat glanced uneasily at the flask in LaFleur's hand. "Oh, I know it's not strictly allowed," LaFleur said, "bringing in outside liquor. But I need help. Ethan said you were the expert in these parts when it comes to Pappy."

"You've got me interested," said Lat, "but I have no idea where you're going with this."

"Would you take a taste of the whiskey I've got in this flask, let me know what you think?"

"Sure, I guess so." Lat brought out a shot glass and poured a half a shot, sniffed it carefully, then took a sip. "Okay, what am I supposed to be looking for?"

"How does that compare to your 23-year-old?"

"Oh, no comparison. This is harsh, no feel at all to it, no subtlety."

"How about compared to the Rip Van Winkle?"

Lat raised the shot glass again, looked at it closely. "Right color." He took another sniff. "Not a bad nose." Took a sip. "Nope. Not awful, but not Pappy, not even the Rip."

"But could it be passed off as Pappy, to the unsuspecting?"

"Oh, sure. I'll be honest, most of the guys who buy this stuff, they're doing it to impress someone—their friends, a client, whatever—they may have never even had it before, or even if they had, wouldn't be able to tell the difference."

"That's almost exactly what Ethan said."

"Where'd you get that, anyway? And why did you think it was Pappy?"

"The proverbial long story." He reached into his coat again, this time bringing out a photo clipped from a newspaper. "I'm a retired detective, out here from New York. I've gotten involved in an investigation into what appears to be a counterfeit whiskey operation here in Montana."

"Well, I can confirm that what you've got there isn't Pappy."

"That brings me to my second question." He held out the photo. "Not to be too melodramatic about it, but have you ever seen this woman?"

Lat looked down at the photo and answered immediately. "Sure. That's Brenda Clark. She worked here, briefly. She was a great bartender, really knew her way around a bottle of whiskey. Especially the bourbons; we get some pretty high-rollers in here at times, and she was always able to suggest exactly the right thing." He frowned. "Unfortunately, she flaked out."

"What do you mean?"

"She just left, unannounced. She was here one day, seemed happy, doing a great job; the next night she didn't show up for work."

"Wait. This is Kyla Macdonald?" I asked.

"Exactly. But Lat couldn't really tell us much about her. She had used an assumed name, and stayed on as his late shift bartender for just under a week. Like I said, she left the McAllister without notice. This was apparently her first stop."

"How did you track her down from there?"

"Lat had heard shortly after she'd left that a new female bartender at the Gravel Bar had come and gone quickly, after working there only a few days. It sounded like her, so that's where I went next."

70

Gravel Bar

"Yeah, she was here," said Tyler, the bar manager, pointing to the newspaper clipping in LaFleur's hand. "I hired her for the late shift. Worked two days, then disappeared without a word. I should have known she'd be trouble."

"Why is that?" asked LaFleur, folding the article and putting it back into his coat pocket. He'd made quick friends with the bartender a little earlier, then asked to talk to the manager, on 'business.' He used his position as a bar and restaurant owner to establish some credibility, then shifted the conversation to the search for Kyla, cleverly avoiding any explicit reasons for his curiosity. The manager was more interested in talking about his own problems than worrying about who LaFleur was or why he was asking questions, a common trait LaFleur routinely counted on.

"Oh, she seemed flighty right from the start. Right away started to ask strange questions, like who are my distributors, what do I pay for this and that, who buys the expensive stuff, things like that. None of your business, I said, just serve up what's ordered and smile a lot."

"Did she say where she was going?"

"Didn't even say she was leaving."

"And you said her name was…?"

"Maggie Halloran. But that's another thing, she didn't have any ID on her, she claimed to have lost her purse, and just hadn't had time to get to the DMV to get a replacement driver's license. After she split, I checked, and the social she gave me was bogus, too. But I hired her anyway; she did seem to know her stuff, and nights are hard to fill."

"You said she was interested in 'the expensive stuff.' Did she give any indication as to what she might mean by that?"

"Whiskey. She was really interested in what kinds of whiskey we served."

"What do you serve the most of?"

"Local Montana beers; that's what we're known for."

"Spirits, I mean."

"Oh, lots of Jack and Coke, Captain and Coke, that sort of thing."

"What about shots?"

"The usual suspects. Maker's Mark, Bulleit, Knob Creek."

"Pappy?"

"Now, that's interesting. She was always on about Pappy Van Winkle. Especially the rare stuff."

"Do you have any on hand?"

"I did have some, just a couple of bottles. Got a deal on it. It sold out quickly, and I meant to get more of it in, but haven't gotten around to it. It was a good seller, though. I'm going to stock it, just haven't talked to my distributor about it."

"Is that where you got the Pappy, from your regular distributor?"

Tyler looked around uncomfortably before answering. "No, it wasn't from my regular guy; it was somebody who just came in one day, working a new region, he said, trying to drum up business. Foreigner, talked funny."

"Good price, you said?"

"An incredible price; low enough that I didn't question it. I know Pappy is hard to get, so I jumped on it."

"Did you ever see this distributor again? Has he followed up, looking for more orders?"

"Nope. Haven't seen him since. He did say he'd be back, though he didn't leave a card, which seems strange, now that I think of it."

"Yes, that does seem odd. Anyway, like I said, I'm thinking of relocating out here and can use all the free advice I can get. If this Pappy reseller comes by again, can you let me know?"

"Sure. Where are you thinking about setting up?"

"Oh, still scouting locations. I heard the bar up in Norris might be available."

"Nope, already been closed down, I heard. Anyway, no market for Pappy there, I can tell you that."

"No?"

"Coors, Coors Light, Bud, Bud Light, Miller, Miller Light. That's what sold in Norris."

As LaFleur got up to leave, thanking the bartender for the information, the bartender raised his hand to stop him. "Say, I almost forgot to mention, talking about the booze and all, an odd thing

72

about that woman, this so-called Margaret, Maggie whatever, Halloran?"

"What was that?"

"You're not the first one to come in asking about her."

LaFleur's eyebrows went to the roof. "No?"

"Just before she scrammed, some guy came in, another foreigner—getting more of them up here lately—wanting to know where she'd gone. I told him the same thing I just told you."

"How do you know so much about Kyla?" I asked, as LaFleur fixed two floaters at the bar. "And what she was working on? It sounds like she didn't let anyone know who she was."

"Mainly from Mary. Apparently, Kyla had gotten very close to her in the short time she was working at the Pony, and had confided in her to some extent. Not concerning the investigation, of course, but her personal situation. Mary never came out and said it, but it sounded like Kyla had been having a pretty rough time as a newly single mom. Domestic abuse, probably. Then there had been trouble at her previous job on the Cincinnati police force, not to mention the challenges related to Ailsa's learning difficulties.

"Then after everything was wrapped up, I took a trip out to Cincinnati to visit Kyla's mother and daughter. I couldn't stand the thought of them not knowing the real story, how Kyla had been so instrumental in breaking things open. And how much more important it had been than just counterfeit whiskey.

"It's too bad she never lived to see the result."

The Bale of Hay

VIRGINIA CITY, MONTANA

A couple of casual conversations while sitting at the bar at the Gravel led LaFleur to his next stop, the Bale of Hay Saloon in Virginia City, about twenty minutes west of Ennis on MT-287.

A veritable preserved ghost town, Virginia City gets a lot of tourist traffic during the summer. It's also the Madison County seat, so official business lunches are often held in the local bars. LaFleur thought it was worth a try. The Bale of Hay bills itself as the oldest bar in Montana—which is true, in the sense that it is the bar with the earliest (known) founding date of 1863. It has not, however, been in continuous operation all those years. Still, a historic site. They also claim to be haunted, something LaFleur put no stock in whatsoever. Very rustic inside and out—tin ceiling, rough wooden floors, dark wood on the walls.

He'd learned from Lat that the bar had been closed for some time, only recently reopened under the new ownership of a local fellow, Jay Cowan. Cowan had an interesting history himself. A Virginia City resident and author, he had been close friends with the gonzo writer Hunter S. Thompson, even acting as property manager and living on his property in Aspen for some time.

After waiting for a lull in the activity at the bar, LaFleur ordered a Famous Grouse and struck up a conversation with the barman, whose name, he learned, was Monroe, but please call me Morrie. No, Jay wasn't around today, he informed LaFleur, to his disappointment.

"Just some water on the side, please," he said as Morrie set his drink down. "Say, I'm surprised you have Grouse on hand. Get much call for it?"

"No, not really," Morrie replied. "Not a lot of Scotch drinkers in general, these parts. Bourbon and rye, that's the thing."

"A friend was just telling me I should get off Scotch. Gave me the tired old 'tastes like medicine' complaint, and said I need to learn to appreciate a good bourbon. Whiskey spelled with an 'e,' he says, is the only real whiskey."

"All a matter of taste," Morrie said, diplomatically.

"Well, I'll tell you, I've tried it, and I just don't get it. Not to sound too much like my friend, but bourbon tastes like mouthwash to me."

"Maybe you haven't tried the right one," Morrie countered. "Not all whiskies are born equal, you know."

"Nor are all Scotches, I realize that. But bourbon is just too, I don't know, too sweet, somehow."

"You just haven't tried the right one," Morrie repeated.

"I'll admit I haven't tried what would be called a 'top shelf' bourbon. What would you recommend?"

Morrie's sudden look of happy expectation gave LaFleur the impression that he was about to be had. But what Morrie said next floored him.

"Have I got the thing for you! Pappy Van Winkle!"

LaFleur chuckled softly to himself as Morrie turned away to get a bottle from the shelf. Always better to let the mark think it was his idea.

"Here you go!" say Morrie, as he held the bottle out to LaFleur with a flourish. "Pappy Van Winkle Family Reserve, 23 Year Old. Liquid gold!"

LaFleur held the bottle out in front of him. "Very impressive looking, I'll say that. But…I don't know…liquid gold? Is it very expensive?"

Morrie became more expansive than ever. "Normally, yes. Very. Thousands of dollars a bottle. If you can get it at all. Places back in New York City, they sell this stuff for hundreds of dollars a shot. A shot, mind you!"

LaFleur put the bottle down with exaggerated care. "Ouch! No, not for me. I'll stick to Scotch."

Morrie leaned over. "Listen. I'm in a position here to do you a favor. Normally we charge one-fifty a shot. A lot less than some others around here charge, if they can even get their hands on it, that is. But I'll let you in on something—I know this won't go any further—"

LaFleur nodded in assent.

"Jay didn't pay thousands for this. You have to stay open to opportunity when it knocks, know what I mean? So, a few weeks ago, I'm tending, Jay is in back. A guy comes in, foreign, Russian, maybe, had an odd accent. Anyway, wants to see the manager, he says he's a new rep for a distillery back east, and he's having a hard time. I called Jay out and the guy gives him a spiel. He's missing his quotas, the boss back at the home office is hounding him day and night. He says he's got to get his numbers up or he's finished. Hard luck, right? Then he says he's desperate, and needs a sale, no matter what it takes. But then we find out it's Pappy that he's trying to move. Well, Jay tells him, I can't afford it, there's just not a big enough market around here. But the guy says he's willing to take a big loss, personally, and hide it in his report, so he can report a sale and keep his job. So, Jay goes for it." Morrie leaned forward. "I'll make you a deal. It would make your friend happy, right, to get you turned on to a real whiskey?"

La Fleur smiled, shaking his head slightly. "I don't know. Not sure it's worth it."

"A hundred bucks. What do you say?"

LaFleur smiled again, quickly deciding to take advantage of the offer. "Oh, sure, what the hell," he said. *Might be a waste of money, but it's the first real chance I've had; better take it.*

Morrie brought out a shot glass and filled it about three-quarters of the way full, maybe half an ounce shy of a standard shot. *No matter*, thought LaFleur, *that's good enough for my purposes.*

He took a careful sip, then widened his eyes in mock surprise. "Very good!"

Another customer came in and required Morrie's attention, so he stepped away, down to the other end of the bar. LaFleur quickly reached into his coat pocket and surreptitiously brought out his flask. He poured a small amount into the stainless-steel cap, while holding it out of sight under the bar, tasted it, then put the cap back on and replaced the flask in his coat. He tasted the Pappy on the bar in front of him again.

The two were identical.

After a couple of minutes, Morrie came back over. "What do you think? Are you a convert?"

"That's clearly better than any other whiskey I've tried. I still don't think I'd pay that much for it."

"Oh, they make a whole range of Pappy. Here," he said, turning around towards the bar, "want to try a Rip Van Winkle? Only forty dollars."

"No, now that you've spoiled me with the good stuff, I don't want to ruin the experience. Thanks for letting me try it, by the way."

"No problem. Anyway, I'm pretty sure this guy's going to come back. I'll give you the same deal, next time you come in."

"I appreciate that," he said, warmly. He reached into his coat again, this time to bring out the newspaper clipping—a good time to take advantage of the good will he'd just paid for, he figured. "I'm a bit embarrassed to ask you this," he said, "but could you take a look at this picture? I'm trying to locate someone, a woman." He paused. "It's a long story, a personal thing. I'd rather not go in to the details…" He trailed off.

Morrie took a look at the photo, then looked up at LaFleur. "Are you kidding me?"

LaFleur frowned. "Why?"

"I've seen her. She came in here two or three times, it was a week, maybe ten days ago. And I have to tell you, this seems like a hell of a coincidence."

"I'm not sure I know what you mean."

"All she ever ordered was a shot of Pappy. The twenty-three-year old Reserve you just tried. Now don't tell me that's not a coincidence, you showing up here with her picture. Right after you trying the same Pappy?" Morrie shook his head in wonderment. "Boy, that takes the cake, huh?"

LaFleur gave a slight sigh of relief as he realized that Morrie wasn't going to question his motives for asking about the photo. "Have you seen her since?" he asked.

"Nope. She just came in, like I said, twice, ordered the expensive Pappy both times."

"Did she say anything about where she was going?"

"Not a word. She did seem friendly, though. Struck up a conversation with a couple of other customers, but didn't stay long either time."

LaFleur folded the clipping and put it away. "Well, thanks anyway."

"Sure." Morrie started back towards the other end of the bar to tend to his other customer. He stopped and looked over at LaFleur for a moment.

"Hope you find her," he said.

"So that's where you went next, A.C., to Pony?" I asked.

"I didn't know anything about the Pony Bar at this point," LaFleur replied. "That would come the next day. No, my next stop was a place a little farther down the road from Virginia City, a place called Chick's, in Alder."

"By the way, what's happening back in Moonlight while you are out on the road?"

"That was a problem; it made me very nervous to be away. And since I'd told Doc not to make or take any cell calls, I didn't have a good way to stay in contact with him. All I could do was email a couple of times from my phone, which I really didn't know how to do very well—a phone was a phone to me, not a camera or a computer or a sound system. It's all changed now, of course; the phones we had in those days were like Babylonian stone tablets compared to what we have now. Even I rely on my iPhone implant now, something that I never saw coming, I'll tell you. The heads-up display, though; I just can't get the hang of that. Anyway, I was able to find out that everyone at the house was still safe and secure, and that nothing had changed as far as the sheriff's investigation."

"You'd been away for less than a day so far, right? So, you wouldn't have expected anything to have changed."

"Not with the official investigation, no. But we felt that the threat to Doc, and by extension, to everyone in the house, was a clear and present danger, as they say. It made me very uneasy, so knowing they hadn't heard or seen anything unusual was a big relief. I still knew that the quicker I could come up with something, the better."

"That's understandable. By the way, your recollection of these events is remarkable. How do you remember all of this?"

"Before you came, I got out my old notes and went through them."

"You've kept your notes all this time?"

"Never know when I might want to write a book," he replied, and then laughed. "Although that's more in Doc's line."

Chick's Bar

ALDER, MONTANA

There was quite a commotion at the bar when LaFleur walked into Chick's—several patrons gathered around the front of the long, curving bar, yelling and carrying on. As he got closer, he could see money being laid down on the bar, as a tall cowboy adjusted his hat, spread his arms wide, then leaned over to the bar and reached out with something in his hand. LaFleur couldn't quite see what was going on, so edged around to the left end of the bar, where another group had congregated.

Just as he neared the group, he looked over to the front of the bar and saw the cowboy launch a small, toy car in his direction, against the tall rounded edge that ran along the entire front of the bar. The car rolled to a stop in front of LaFleur's group, to the sound of much celebration.

It took him a few minutes to understand what was going on, at least the rudiments—it was some sort of betting game, the winner being the one who rolled his or her car closest to the finish line marked at the left end of the bar. Or something like that.

In any event, money changed hands, and everyone was apparently having a great time. At this point someone noticed LaFleur standing back from the crowd and urged him to come over.

"Come on up! Take a shot at it!"

Several others joined in, but LaFleur resisted the invitations with a good-natured, "Boy, you'll bet on anything around here!"

The tall cowboy walked over and stuck out his hand. "Welcome to Chick's," he said, grandly. "I'm Harlan, I run this here game." LaFleur shook his hand and replied, "They call me A.C.; glad to meet you."

"Now, don't tell me you're not a gambling man," Harlan chided him.

"Oh, no, it's not that," LaFleur replied. "I'm a gambler. Just not much of a driver."

Harlan laughed, then pointed to a poker table over in the corner by the front door. "Well, then, how about some Texas Hold'em?

Friday nights, we always have a game going. Should be starting up in about an hour."

"Now that's more like it!" said LaFleur. "Count me in."

"Okay, then! In the meantime, have Jenny there fix you up with something to drink." He called to the barmaid. "Jenny! New customer. The first one's on me!"

After thanking Harlan, LaFleur settled in to a spot on the far right of the bar, away from the racing competition. As he sat down, he scanned the rows of liquor bottles behind the bar, looking for Pappy, or anything high-end. It appeared that the Chick's crowd didn't go in for that kind of thing; there was, however, a larger than usual lineup of Fireball, Jaegermeister, and various flavored vodkas and rums.

Jenny was a bright young thing, her hair tied in pigtails with blue-checked ribbons and wearing a Lyle Lovett t-shirt. LaFleur was immediately charmed.

Over the course of two Scotch and waters (not Grouse, unfortunately), LaFleur learned that: one, Chick's (like many rural Montana restaurant/bars) had very nice rooms out back, one of which Jenny booked for him for that night, as it was late and there was poker ahead; and two, she'd never heard of Pappy Van Winkle, and even asked around at the bar, and reported that no one there had ever heard of it; and three, she didn't recognize the woman in the photo.

While talking with Jenny, LaFleur had noticed a large number of extremely well-done color portraits hanging on the wall behind him.

"Oh, yes," said Jenny. "Those are all local residents, done by a woman who lives nearby. They're remarkable, aren't they?"

LaFleur agreed, marveling at yet another unexpected aspect of Madison County culture.

"Excuse me a minute, Jenny? I need to make a call."

"Sure thing."

LaFleur remembered just in time that he couldn't call Fuentes while he was lying low. He called Maggie instead—it was really her he needed to talk to, anyway, he realized.

"Everything going okay upstairs?" he asked, as soon as she had answered. He listened to her long reply, nodding to himself periodically.

"Okay," he said, "let me know if there's any change."

The poker game that night was both surprising and about what he'd expected. Surprising in that the stakes were higher than he'd thought they'd be—two and five dollar blinds, no limit—and expected in that the cowboys played like, well, like cowboys, raising seemingly randomly, calling with trash and hitting on the river, in effect playing more like they were playing video poker than serious poker. LaFleur played for almost three hours, finally lost about forty dollars, (which took some careful money management—it was better to lose a little than win and make an impression—he didn't particularly want to be remembered), and then went to bed.

The forty dollars lost at poker and the seventy-five for the motel room was money well spent. With the judicious use of table talk, he was able to determine that there was absolutely no action in Pappy going on at Chick's, or in the small towns to the north, Sheridan and Twin Bridges. So, he'd all but confirmed that this was outside the area of the distribution of the fake whiskey and now could concentrate his efforts elsewhere.

And one of the cowboys had let something else useful slip—he'd heard in Virginia City recently that if you want really good whiskey at a bargain price, go to Pony.

The Famous Pony Bar

PONY, MONTANA

Late the next morning, after an excellent but too-big Montana breakfast at Chick's restaurant, almost rivaling one of Big Frank's, LaFleur retraced his path back through Virginia City and Ennis. Continuing north on 287 through McAllister, in a few minutes he was at Norris. In the interest of completeness, he'd originally intended to stop in, but the place was boarded up. Must not have sold enough Bud Light. Probably would have been a waste of time. Ethan told him later that the building had been bought by a Moonlight member named John Sampson, who'd immediately closed the place down, then removed the big wooden bar and moved it to his fishing ranch, the Madison Double R. He'd also needed the liquor license.

Ten more minutes brought him to Harrison and the turnoff to Pony. And fifteen minutes after that, he was there. He drove to the end of town. He could see that the road ahead petered out into a dirt track, so turned around at a wide spot at a gate off to the right. Driving back down the street, he could tell that this place was special; Virginia City was much larger, and obviously the buildings there were original, as they were here, but the main street of Pony, Broadway, seemed more authentic, somehow.

He pulled off to the side of the road next to an old wooden building with an American flag out front and a bleached-white steer's skull mounted in the center of the sloping porch roof. A small white sign with faded black and red lettering stuck out from the side of the building above the skull.

Pony Bar, it said.

"I met Mary at the Pony, you know," I said. "She convinced Dr. Fuentes to tell me the story, or I wouldn't be here now, talking with you."

"Doc told me. Mary's quite something, isn't she?"

"I can only imagine. I met her just that once, and we never really had a chance to talk, but still, she impressed me. She seems to be a very strong woman."

"When you get back to Montana, arrange to meet with her again, in Pony or at her home in Harrison. I'm sure she'd love to talk to you. I can give you an overview of what I learned that day at the Pony, but much of the real story of what happened should come from her. She made a lot of it happen. Well, besides Kyla, of course."

Three wooden signs hung above the front door to the Pony Bar. The oldest and roughest simply had the words "Pony Bar" carved into the smooth face of a split log. The other two were newer, of what looked like redwood. The first declared in large black letters that "FREEDOM is not FREE," and underneath that a smaller sign identified the building as VFW POST 3831.

My kind of folks, LaFleur thought as he went in.

The interior was just about as he had imagined it, having gotten a good taste of Montana bar décor the previous day—posters, signs, local paraphernalia, paintings, and beer advertisements plastered the walls and ceiling. A long wooden bar ran the full length of the room on the left; on the right were three of the video gaming machines so ubiquitous to Montana bars; and against the back wall, a small table and three metal stools, the only table in the place. As he moved toward the back of the bar, he saw a large passthrough cut into the wall next to the bottle shelf behind the bar, opening into another room with a pool table.

The selection of liquor behind the bar was typical of what he'd seen so far—flavored rums, common specialty liquors, a standard assortment of gin, vodka, and Scotch, a couple of rye whiskeys, and the usual bourbons: Ten High, Jim Beam, Jack Daniels. At first glance, an unremarkable selection, except for two things—the surprising lack of Fireball, and, prominently displayed, several bottles of Pappy Van Winkle, Family Reserve, 23 Year Old.

Jackpot.

There was only one seat open at the bar, near the end. The three end stools themselves were occupied by two older men and a matronly looking woman. All three had a bottle of beer in front of them.

"Mind if I join you?" asked LaFleur, easing onto the seat.

"Not at all!" said the woman, brightly. She leaned back, stretching her hand behind her two companions. LaFleur leaned over and shook it. "I'm Mary."

"Glad to meet you," replied LaFleur. "I'm A.C. LaFleur."

"This is Carl, next to me, and John, next to you," Mary said, gesturing to each in turn. Carl and John both nodded a hello and murmured a glad to meet you.

"Glad to meet you all," said LaFleur. "Do you live here in Pony?"

"Oh, no," Mary replied. "We live down in Harrison. You came through it on your way here, right at the intersection of 287 and 283. My late husband and I retired there—of all places—many years ago."

"The intersection is just past the high school," Carl added. "The big white building right there on the road."

"Oh, yes, I remember seeing that."

"Go Wildcats," said John.

"We come up here to the Pony every Saturday, at noon," explained Mary. "Have been for years. It's sort of a tradition, I guess you'd call it. We each have four bottles of beer, then go home."

LaFleur smiled. "Sounds like a wonderful tradition." He looked over at their beer bottles. "Looks like you are about ready for another one," he said. "I hope you haven't had your quota of four yet—I'd like to buy you a round."

"Oh, no," said Mary, frowning. "That wouldn't be right, you being new here and all." Carl and John shook their heads in agreement.

"Well, I'll admit I have an ulterior motive," LaFleur said. "I was hoping to get some information in return." Mary's frown deepened, and Carl and John looked over at him suspiciously. 'Oh, I have absolutely the best intentions," he said hastily. "Let me explain."

The three of them looked at one another, and after a few seconds seemed to come to some sort of silent agreement. "Okay," said Mary, obviously the spokesperson for the group. "Go ahead."

He briefly related his reasons for coming to the Pony—the basic details of the incident in Moonlight, his background and the reasons for his getting involved in the investigation, and even some of the previous days' activities. He then convinced them to let him buy their third round, and appeared to have gained their confidence.

When it came to the subject of the unusual presence in the bar of so much high-end Pappy Van Winkle, they seemed unsurprised at his suspicions, and willing to talk about it.

"You're exactly right to wonder about that," Carl said. "From what we understand from Walt, the owner, he's getting it at a very good price. We've heard that stuff is very top shelf."

"Hoity-toity," said Mary.

"And hard to get," said Carl, "and normally very expensive, so it is unusual."

"That's right," John said. "And that's not the only unusual thing happening around here," he added.

"What do you mean?"

"The fellows that have been selling the Pappy Van Winkle to Walt moved into the big empty houses on North Willow Creek not long ago, and set up some sort of operation there. Pretty big, from the looks of it. There's a lot of traffic in and out, always a big white Mercedes van. Soon after they got here, they started handing out free stuff to everyone, ceramic figurines, Christmas ornaments, all sorts of different things, and all of it done—they say—using 3-D printing." He pointed to a small porcelain-colored horse figurine behind the bar. "That's one of theirs."

LaFleur leaned forward to get a closer look. "Very nice. I didn't know 3-D printing had gotten that sophisticated."

"Oh, they claim they have a brand-new process, 'state-of-the-art,' they said. And they say that once they get past the experimental stage, they're going to go into full production mode. Pretty soon now, they said."

"Could mean jobs, right here in Pony," said Carl. "Or so they claim."

"They're doing this here in Pony?" asked LaFleur.

"Right up the road, at the edge of town. It's an old estate, been empty for years. Two big old Victorian houses and an outbuilding, a sort of barn."

"And the whiskey? They're making that here, too?"

"Don't know about that," said Mary. "They just told us they're making the ceramic stuff over there."

"About the whiskey," said LaFleur, after a moment's reflection. "Do you think Walt would let me sample it?"

'Heck, we don't need to ask Walt," said John. He called to the barmaid. "Molly! Give us a shot of the Pappy, will you?"

Molly turned out to be a delightful young woman, bright and outgoing, with long red hair and a butterfly tattooed on her neck. LaFleur was told later that she was a real favorite with the locals, who all dreaded the day, fast approaching, when she would go back down to Montana State in Bozeman to finish her degree in architecture, probably never to return to Pony.

"Here you go, John," she said, putting the shot glass down in front of him.

"Oh, no, this is for Mr. LaFleur, here. He's a detective," he added, a bit dramatically.

"Oh, exciting! Are you on a case?"

"Actually, yes," LaFleur replied. "This is research," he added with a smile.

He picked up the shot of Pappy. A quick taste confirmed that it matched the fake Pappy from Kyla's carry-on. "I understand you're selling a lot of this lately."

"Flying off the shelf," said Molly. "But at the price we're charging, it's not surprising."

"Know anything about the supplier?"

"You mean those guys up at the mansion? Nope. They're sort of a mysterious bunch, wouldn't you say, guys?" John, Carl, and Mary all agreed. "But look at this ceramic doo-hickey they gave me the other day." She took a small, intricate object from the shelf behind her and put it on the bar in front of LaFleur. "Awesome, huh?"

LaFleur picked it up carefully, surprised at the weight and apparent strength of what had at first glance appeared to be a very delicate, filigreed ornament. "Very impressive," he said. "Did they tell you what it's made of?"

"No. Unbreakable, they said. Part of a new process, very experimental."

"That's what they've told all of us," John said, "just like I said before, Mr. LaFleur."

"Yes, that's right, you did, John. Well, thanks a lot, Molly."

"Sure thing."

As Molly walked away, a couple of younger men—ranch hands, by the looks of them—came up and greeted Mary and her two companions. While they talked, LaFleur stared down at his beer bottle and tried to make some sense of what he'd been hearing.

I sensed that there was something important coming, but couldn't see it quite yet. "Okay, there must be a connection," I said. "But what does 3-D printing have to do with counterfeit Pappy Van Winkle?"

"That's a very good question. And one that Kyla answered. That is, she found part of the answer, but without knowing it. And it went beyond the Pappy, as you've guessed. Unfortunately for Kyla, far beyond."

It was at least fifteen minutes before LaFleur got a chance to talk again with the Pony Gang (as he'd subconsciously started to think of them), but hadn't come up with a thing.

Maybe it was time to ask about Kyla. He got out the newspaper photo and handed it to John.

"Have any of you ever seen this woman?" he asked.

John looked at it, then handed it to Carl, who glanced at it, looked over at Mary, started to say something, then handed her the photo. Mary studied it for about thirty seconds, then turned to her friends.

"Don't you recognize her?" she asked. She gave the picture back to Carl, who held it up so he and John could both look at it. After a minute, Mary reached over and tapped the front of the photo with a forefinger.

"It's Margaret!" she told them, emphatically. "Margaret from last week!"

"By God, I believe you're right, Mary," said Carl. "Her hair is a lot different in this photo."

"It's not a good picture of her, at all, Mr. LaFleur," said John. "But Mary's right, that's sure Margaret."

"Her real name is Kyla Macdonald," said LaFleur.

Mary gasped. "Oh, my gosh, it's the poor woman who was killed at the airport in Bozeman."

"We didn't recognize her on the news," said John. "She'd changed her hair again since she'd been here, or something."

"And we only saw her just the one time," added John.

"So, she was here, then?" LaFleur reached over and took the picture back from Carl. "For how long? Was she working here?"

"Well, we met her when we were up here last Saturday," Mary told him. "She said she'd been working here just a few days, on the late shift, and had come in to talk to Walt. She seemed to be very anxious to talk to him, but only waited around for maybe half an hour, then left. We never saw her again, and Walt said she never showed up for work after that night. Oh, my gosh, how terrible. She was such a nice woman."

"Did you get a chance to talk with her about anything else? Did she tell you what she was doing here?"

"She just said she was here temporarily, had become stranded in Three Forks somehow—not sure she ever said how exactly—and was trying to earn enough money to get back east," said Mary. "She said she had a daughter back there that she was trying to get back to. Must have been having some sort of domestic trouble, I guess. She didn't say much more than that."

"She knew an awful lot about whiskey, though," said John, "especially Pappy Van Winkle."

"That's right," agreed Carl, "and she seemed pretty interested in what was happening up at the house on North Willow Creek."

"Molly said a few minutes ago that she thought the men at the mansion were 'a mysterious bunch,' and you all agreed. Can you tell me why you think that?"

"Well, they're foreign," said John, "not that there's anything wrong with that," he quickly amended, "but foreign in a sort of unfriendly way, if you know what I mean. Real standoffish."

"That's right," agreed Carl. "Whenever they come in here, they gather at a table all to themselves, talking together in whatever language it is, and act kind of bossy. Rude. Sort of belligerent. Moving our coats and taking over a table without asking, that sort of thing."

"How many of them are there?"

"Three, but one time a fourth guy joined them; he didn't stay around long.

"Have they caused any trouble?"

"Other than that sort of stuff? No, I guess not, not really. But they just don't act like regular businessmen, or engineers, which they claim to be."

"Doug is awful suspicious," offered Carl.

"Doug?" LaFleur asked.

"Oh, a friend of ours who lives here in Pony. He doesn't like it one bit. Doesn't believe there's going to be any jobs. Or anything else good to come out of it. We think he's probably right."

"Yeah, Doug has been very vocal about his dislike of the whole situation," chimed in John. "He came close to starting a fight one day, remember Carl?"

"Yeah, that's right; but Doug's been very touchy in general, lately. I hear they even banned him from the Harrison ball games this summer for harassing the umpire." He shook his head in sympathy, it appeared. "But anyway, yeah, he really doesn't like them."

"We hope he's wrong," said Mary. "Still, it is all pretty mysterious." She took a sip of her beer. "But I can't help thinking about that poor girl," she said. "Killed like that." She gave LaFleur a hard look. "You said you're investigating her murder?"

"Yes, along with the shooting in Moonlight; we think they could be related. We're still trying to come up with some hard evidence."

"Well, if there's anything we can do to help, you be sure and let us know."

I had been thinking about the puzzle of the 3-D printing all the while LaFleur related his encounter with the Pony Gang.

"Okay," I said. "This might be a long shot, but—I remember a story about wine counterfeiting from a few years ago. Along with the wine itself, and the label, isn't there also something about the glass? The bottle, I mean? How the bottle is embossed, or made, or something like that?"

"Very astute, Reagan. As the case unfolded, we learned a lot about wine and liquor counterfeiting, and yes, the chemical and radioactive components of the wine, the age and composition of the paper and ink of the label, the state of the cork, all are factors, and even if reproduced expertly, the bottle is sometimes the give-away. For example, four bottles of Laffite originally owned by Thomas Jefferson, with the initials 'Th.J.' etched on the bottles, were sold at auction several years ago to a billionaire investor. He paid tens of thousands of dollars each. It looked exactly right: wine, cork, label, everything. The etching later proved to be modern. They were counterfeit." He paused, sipping his Grouse, which was certainly authentic, straight from the Glenturrit distillery in Scotland. "But you're getting ahead of the story again."

"But I'm dying to know what Kyla found. She was so resourceful, so determined. I just want to know what she did." I couldn't help letting out a long sigh. "What she did that got her killed."

Presents for Ailsa

THREE FORKS, MONTANA

After spending most of the day in Pony, LaFleur drove up to Three Forks. According to Mary, the Travelodge at the intersection of I-90 and highway 287 was where Kyla had been staying for the few days she'd worked at the bar.

He almost missed the motel as he drove past the truck stop—the sign by the road was very small and the low, brick building sat far off the highway, hidden by the large fuel bays. He turned off into the large truck parking area just past the motel and drove slowly back. As he pulled up to the front and parked, he felt a chill. *This is where she spent her last hours. Pretty bleak.*

He shook off his dark feelings and went into the lobby. The receptionist was a dark-haired young woman of about twenty, sporting the inevitable shoulder tattoo and what he guessed was a rhinestone nose pin. LaFleur kept his first bad impression to himself—*who told you that was attractive?* As it turned out, the girl was pleasant, articulate, and quite helpful. *Who could tell, these days? Guess I'm getting old.*

He pulled out the picture of Kyla he'd been showing around. "I know you are not allowed to divulge personal information on guests, but perhaps you could help me out. Maybe you've heard about the murder that took place in the Bozeman airport parking lot a few days ago?"

The girl nodded. "Yes, I saw something about that on the news the other night. Why?"

"I'm a detective—well, retired now, actually—but I'm helping out a friend," he said, guessing that she would presume he had some kind of official sanction. "He's asked me to check into her last known whereabouts, and we believe that she stayed here at the Travelodge for several days." He handed her the photo. "Do you remember her?"

She looked down at the picture and gasped. "Oh, my gosh, that's her! That's the woman who was here! I didn't pay much attention to the report on TV, but now that I see her close up, yes, that's her. She stayed here several days, like you said." She picked up the clipping and looked at it again. "Yes, that's her. In fact, she left some things behind in her room."

"What did she leave behind, exactly? Anything that looked business related?"

"No, it was just some personal items. Things she'd bought recently, it looked like, kid's books and some clothes, still in the bags. They were sort of behind the bed by the wall. We were going to send them to her, but it's the strangest thing—the address she gave was the Pony Bar, you know, in Pony? And now that I think of it," she said as she picked up the newspaper clipping again, "I don't recognize her name, either."

"She didn't leave any contact information? Address? Cell phone number?"

"No, nothing. I guess the night clerk wasn't too careful about checking her in," she finished, apologetically.

LaFleur pondered that for a moment. *Kyla was certainly being careful, herself. Did she already know that she was in danger?* "Can I take a look at the items she left?" he asked. "There might be something there we can use."

"I suppose that would be all right," the girl replied. "Just a minute, they're just there in the office."

She returned a minute later with two white plastic bags. "This is what we found in her room," she said, handing the bags over the counter.

"Thanks. I'll just sit here in the lobby."

"That's fine."

LaFleur took the bags and sat down on the large leather couch opposite the reception desk. In the first bag were two children's books, both with book award stickers on the front cover, both about young girls making their own way in life. *How old did Doc say the daughter was, nine?* The books looked a bit advanced for that age, especially if she had learning issues. But of course, that didn't mean she wasn't very intelligent, he reminded himself. He'd been through something similar with one of his own daughters.

He opened the second bag and found two brightly colored shirts, one a souvenir T-shirt, purple with a pink moose on the front, the other a red-and-blue checked cowgirl style shirt with pearl snaps. *Bet she'd love them.*

He carefully put the items back in the bags and took them over to the reception desk.

"I'd like to take these with me, if that's alright. I can get them to her family."

"Well, I'm not sure…"

"Listen. I'll leave you my card; you can contact me any time if there's a problem. I'll be here in the area for the next couple of weeks."

"Yeah, well, sure, that would be okay," she agreed. She picked his card up off of the desk. "I'll give this to my manager right away," she said, pointedly, just to let him know she wasn't as careless about things as the night clerk had been.

"Thanks very much for your help."

"Sure. I'm sorry about the woman. Was she a friend of yours?"

"No. But I wish she had been."

PART THREE

Early Warning System

LaFleur hadn't been able to stop thinking about it, all the way back to Moonlight.

Kyla had in a very short time infiltrated practically every bar in the local area, and had apparently found the evidence she needed. She must have been on her way back to Kentucky when she was killed, the same day she'd met Mary and her friends.

What had given her away?

But more puzzling was the extreme reaction by whomever had killed her. Ockham's Razor appears to have run out of gas. What Kyla had presumably found was evidence of nothing more than a penny-ante booze scam. A relatively minor liquor violation, probably not even jail time; pay a fine, move on to another location and start up again.

What made that worth murder?

The whole experience at the Travelodge had left him both subdued and angry, two emotions that did not sit well together. Over the past few days, he'd built up a very vivid picture of Kyla. He felt that he'd gotten to know her well, as improbable as that seemed, even to himself. And now that he'd brought Ailsa's undelivered presents home with him, he could almost feel Kyla's absence. But that absence was surely not felt as acutely, he reminded himself, as it must be right now by her mother and daughter.

After lunch the group gathered in the living room. There was much to talk about on both sides, A.C. with his report on what he'd learned while out following in Kyla's tracks.

LaFleur went first, his frustration evident. "Well, I'll be bloody well damned if I understand what's going on here. From what I've been able to figure out, Kyla was probably very close to closing in on whoever is moving the illegitimate Pappy all over the county. Every place she worked she got a little closer. At the same time, no one I talked with seemed all that concerned about it. The bartenders and owners I spoke with accepted, more or less, whatever story they'd been told about why they were being given such a good deal.

97

Of course, there's a lot of looking the other way when it comes to this kind of thing, especially in an area like this. Times out here are hard, the market is small and spread out all over the damn place, and keeping a business going is not easy. So, I imagine there is some willful ignorance at play. But even so, it's just not that big of a deal." He paused. "Nothing that would provoke murder."

"What then?" asked Maggie. "All we have to go on is the fake whiskey."

"Yeah, I know. That's what has me stymied."

"I have something that should help," said Frank. "I asked your computer wizard friend F.T. if he could find anything out on the internet that might be related. He called earlier with some information for us."

"What's he come up with?" asked LaFleur.

"He was able to find a record of electrical usage for the place out on North Willow Creek. There's a hell of a lot of power being sucked up at that place, much more than a year ago. And more than would be indicated by a counterfeit whiskey operation."

"Is there any pattern to it?"

"The usage is heaviest during nighttime hours. And there's no related phone or internet usage, so it's likely not any online operation like gambling or porn. Bitcoin mining is typically centered around big cities, so although possible it's unlikely. And the usage spikes at certain times; with some sort of surveillance we might be able to correlate that with activity there. In any case, there's something power-intensive going on there that bears watching."

"And using more power than would be required to manufacture a few Christmas ornaments."

"Exactly."

"There's something else; F.T. identified a vehicle that came through the lower Jack Creek gate the morning Mike was shot. A black Ford F-150. He checked the member records, there's no one in Moonlight registered for that truck. And get this: it came back out exactly thirty-five minutes after the shooting."

"Any ID? Plates?"

"He said the truck was too mud-splattered; the plates were illegible. But he has set up something very clever—he adapted his AI bot to do something like facial recognition, but for that truck, and if comes through again, his program will generate an alarm. I told him to have the bot send it to your cell phone."

"An early warning system. That sounds perfect."

"I thought you'd like that."

LaFleur nodded in satisfaction. "Maybe now we can finally start to make some real progress."

Doug Was Right All Along...

PONY, MONTANA

Doug Soames was a typical rural Montana character, full of the hard knock ways and no nonsense means that make Montana natives a persevering and tenacious lot. Born and raised in Pony, he'd traveled awhile after graduating from Harrison High, and like many of their graduates went into the armed forces right out of school, in his case the Marines. Following his discharge, he worked at various jobs around the state, and eventually settled back in Pony, working at Harrison Elevator until his retirement. Heavy-set but muscular, always wearing faded Levi's, a long-sleeved Western-style shirt, and an old Harrison Wildcats ball cap, he soon became good friends with Mary, John and Carl, and a fixture on the wooden picnic tables that sat out in front of the Pony Bar during the summer months.

He had been among the first, and the most vocal, of Pony residents who were suspicious of the goings-on at the old Pony Mansion, as the locals referred to the small estate located on North Willow Creek at the edge of town. When the strangers who had taken over the place started handing out free ceramic doodads, he hadn't thought too much about it, at first, anyway. But when they started providing the bar with high-end whiskey at bargain basement prices, and when the big, white utility van began going in and out at odd hours, he really began to wonder what was going on. He just didn't buy into their stories. *Jobs? Here? That'll be the day!*

The attitude of the men working there didn't help. Sure, they were lavish with their little gifts and their spending in the bar, but they never seemed all that friendly. They even seemed a bit surly. He'd tried to start up a conversation with some of them many times, but they never responded. *Could be that they don't speak much English,* he said once, but it was obviously only a half-hearted attempt at being conciliatory.

Then Mary told him about the visit from the detective and that the woman who was killed in Bozeman was Margaret, and that the detective thought it might be related, and Doug exploded. *What the hell is going on around here? I don't like it, Mary, I don't like it a goddam bit!*

NORTH WILLOW CREEK

The gunfire was coming from somewhere up above the red brick house at the end of the road—the "Russki House," Doug had been calling it lately.

It didn't sound like any kind of gunfire Doug was familiar with, and he'd been shooting and hunting these hills all his life. It was a strange, thin "popping" sound, louder than a .22, but nothing like a normal handgun or small rifle.

"I'm going up there," he told Molly.

He left the bar and started up the road, already angry. *Got to be them damned Russkis.*

As he passed by the Willow Road estate, he saw the large white van backed up to the big front doors of the barn, but the doors were closed and he couldn't see anything inside. He edged up the road a little farther and tried to peer in at the big house through the trees. He didn't see any obvious activity, and the other white clapboard house was hidden by trees and bushes. He'd heard that the white house was actually some kind of ballroom, which as far as he knew had not been used in recent history. The previous owners had been a strange bunch themselves, standoffish and aloof. He'd never liked them, either, the few times he'd come across them, but at least they were quiet and kept to themselves. No one had ever had any reason to worry about them. *But this bunch...*

He cut over to the creek and worked his way up through the woods above the house.

The gunfire continued sporadically.

The creek at this time of year had almost no water in it, which made it easy to cross over into denser woods as he came to open areas. There was only one more house on the road before it continued on up to the dead end at the trailhead, and it sat out in the middle of a large bare meadow. He left the creek and moved quickly into the woods behind the house, then continued on. The gunfire had stopped for a while, then started again, off to his left.

About two hundred yards up the hill, in a barren stretch between two large stands of timber, he saw them.

There were two of them, one standing alone with a small pistol in his hand, the other about thirty yards away setting up a target on a cardboard box.

"But all of this is just surmise on your part," I interjected. "You can't know exactly what he did, can you? How he died?"

"No, you're right. Not exactly. But knowing Doug like they did, Mary and the rest of group at the Pony could put together a pretty complete picture of how he would have gone about this. And the police search of the area turned up evidence that there had been target shooting at the site—scraps of paper and cardboard scattered around in a small area, grass trampled down in a path between two spots at about the right distance, things like that. So, we can reconstruct the scene pretty accurately."

"But you had so little to go on!"

"Remember Ockham's Razor? Take the facts you have available and whatever fits best must be the truth, or close to it, anyway. In any case, the details here are not that significant. We know Doug was agitated, and went looking for these guys.

"Unfortunately for him, they weren't hard to find."

Doug came out of the trees with a strident yell. "What the hell is going on here?"

No matter that this kind of activity was not at all uncommon in this part of Montana. Doug would certainly not have been surprised by, or even interested in it, had he not already worked himself into a state of outrage. He would not have been able to explain it himself, had he ever gotten the chance.

His body was found later that afternoon, face down in the grass.

DOC'S HOUSE

"Hello, Detective LaFleur?"

"Yes, hello, Mary." Something in her voice alerted him that she was in some distress. "Is everything all right?"

"Oh, Mr. LaFleur, something terrible has happened."

"What's going on, Mary?"

"I can barely stand to say it. Doug—" Her voice broke for a moment, then came back, stronger now. "Doug Soames was found dead about an hour ago."

"Oh, my God, Mary, that's terrible. What—how—where was he found?" he was finally able to get out.

"In the woods just up along North Willow Creek, not far from the edge of town."

"Do you know anything more about what might have happened?"

"From what Molly told me, Doug left the bar in a real agitated state. Lately he's been very vocal about his suspicions about the goings on up there; don't believe anything they say, he always said, don't trust them for a minute, and so on. Anyway, earlier today he told Molly he'd been hearing gun fire from just above the old house, up along the creek somewhere, he thought, and was going up to check it out. When he still hadn't come back after two hours, Molly sent a friend out to look for him—it's not like Doug to miss his evening meal at the Pony, you know. Oh, my," she said as her voice broke again. "Oh, my, I'm sorry." LaFleur waited a moment as she regained her composure. "Well, when the friend came back," she continued, "it was with a deputy. Doug had been shot. Molly called me right away." She paused. "Mr. LaFleur, this is personal now. What can we do to help?"

"Mary, this whole thing is quickly escalating out of control. First Kyla, then the shooting at the golf course, and now Doug. I can't let you get involved."

"We can't let them get away with this!"

"We're working on it. Over the past few days I've learned quite a bit about what Kyla was up to, you know."

"But you told us the other day that you still need evidence."

"We have the whiskey, and with what I've learned—"

"I'm going to call the boys," Mary interrupted, defiantly, "and tell them that we need to get to Pony. Right now. They'll know what to do."

"Mary, please listen to me, you can't go up there. It's too dangerous."

"As far as danger is concerned," said Mary, "what have we got to lose? We're all old, and not all that well. We might not have much longer to go anyway. My AFib and COPD are going to do me in pretty soon. And Carl and John both have serious health problems, too. So, you see, Detective, we're all living on borrowed time, as the saying goes. With what we're already dealing with, what more could we be afraid of?"

"I'm very sorry to hear that," said LaFleur. "But none of that means you should be careless. I don't want any phony courage."

"Detective, what you'll get from us is not phony courage," said Mary, "but Pony courage."

She hung up.

Mary Gets the Goods

THE PONY BAR

They'd been scheming all the way up to Pony. By the time they got there, they had a tentative plan. They were as sure as LaFleur that there was a lot more going on up on North Willow Creek Road than the production of high-tech ornaments. Now they were going to prove it.

They'd seen one of the regulars from the operation in the bar a couple of times before, and quickly confirmed with Molly that he had a fairly regular schedule. He always drove the Sprinter van that constantly went in and out of the North Willow Creek complex.

At their prompting, Molly filled them in on the details of his routine. "Yeah, he's in here a lot. He's always chatting me up. How he thinks he'll get anywhere is beyond me."

"Can we use you as bait?" asked Carl. "Oh, my God, Molly, I'm sorry; that sounded horrible."

"Yes, it did, Carl," said Mary, turning to Molly as she repeated his request. "Can we, Molly?"

"Whatever I can do," Molly said.

"Well, we need a distraction, so you're it," said Mary. "Don't worry, all you need to do is pay a little more attention to him than usual for a few minutes. We'll do the rest."

John had gone up the road to the Willow Creek house to reconnoiter, keeping well out of sight and thinking about Doug all the way. He'd come back in just as Mary and Carl were settling in at their regular spots at the bar.

"We timed it well, John; Molly told us that the driver should be in any time now."

"I don't know," said John. "Looks like there's a lot of activity up there right now," John reported. "No telling how long we'll have to wait."

"No problem," said Carl. "How about a beer?"

As it turned out, they didn't have to wait too long for the driver to show up. He was a young, muscular man about six feet tall with long, greasy, ash-colored hair, Slavic features, and an attitude. Not an engineer type at all. He came in the door with a swagger.

"Molly-dolly," he called out in good but heavily accented English, "it's me, your favorite guy again!"

Molly knew she had to walk a fine line here; she'd been putting this lout off so hard for the past six weeks that if she came on too strong now, he might become suspicious. Time to put that summer stock experience to work. She turned away, waving her hand behind her back—coquettishly, she hoped.

"Ah, Illya (*was that even his real name?* she now wondered), "not now. I'm working."

"Ah, Molly, you are not so busy." He gestured to the three sitting at the far end of the bar. "Only you and me the old folks there, and they look very happy. You are happy, yes, friends?" he called to them.

Mary waved back and smiled. "Sure thing, friend." Carl and John just turned and nodded in his direction.

Illya swung himself up onto a bar stool. "I'll have what your friends are having," he said, tilting his head in their direction.

"No Pappy Van Winkle?" she teased, knowing that they never drank the stuff.

"Oh, no, too good for me! Just a beer."

Molly bent down to the cooler and brought out a longneck Bud. "Here you go, cowboy."

"Ah, yes, the favorite Montana cowboy beer. Very good, Molly!"

Now that she had him in a playful mood, she leaned over to him, elbows on the bar. Her top was not that low cut, but she knew he'd be putting his imagination into overdrive. "Why were you late today? I was beginning to wonder if you were going to show up."

"Oh, busy. You know we are very busy."

"Yes, it seems so. How is that going? Good, I hope?"

Before he could answer, Carl jumped off of his barstool, yelling incoherently. Both Molly and Illya looked over in alarm.

Carl began pointing at John vigorously, yelling repeatedly, "You! You!"

"Calm down, Carl!" John yelled back. "I was only—"

"I know what you were *only*," Carl yelled back. "Now get away from her!"

Illya looked at Molly with amusement and leaned closer to her. "A lover's quarrel?" he asked "Them?" He shook his head and started to turn towards them to get a better look when Carl lurched over and bumped into him, almost knocking him off the stool.

"Hey, old man!" Illya yelled.

Carl immediately backed up, then lurched even closer. "Oh, I'm so sorry," he said, grabbing Illya by the shoulders. "I'm so sorry. Please forgive me." He appeared to lose his balance, grabbing at Illya for support.

"Hey!" Illya cried. "Look out!"

Mary had by now rushed over to them. "Carl, please," she said, pulling him away.

Carl slipped the car keys he'd just lifted from Illya's pocket into her hand, and she slipped out the door.

"That was close," exclaimed Mary, as Molly ushered Illya out the door. Carl had put the keys back into Illya's pocket just as deftly as he'd taken them out. Mary had had just enough time in the van to take pictures for LaFleur, even if she didn't know what she had been taking pictures of.

"He seems to think we have a date," Molly said. "For tonight, but I can't think how he ever got that idea. Guess I'll have to deal with that later." She pursed her lips in concentration. "This is strange," she said. "He said something like, 'it's now or never,' like the old Elvis song? He even hummed a bit of it. Do you think they're getting ready to leave?"

"It sure looked like it to me," said John, "from what I saw up there today. Wouldn't be at all surprised."

"That means we have no time to lose," said Mary. "Which is why we have to get these pictures to Mr. LaFleur ASAP."

In the meantime, LaFleur had gone through Kyla's carry-on bag with the proverbial fine-toothed comb and had found nothing new. No secret pockets, no false bottom, nothing.

Then his phone rang. After a short conversation, he turned to the group. "It was Mary," he said. "She's got evidence."

"Speaking of evidence," I said, "and before you go any further—I'm still curious as to how you know so much about what Kyla was doing. She'd been on the trail of these guys, obviously, but what exactly was she up to? And how did you find out?"

"Good question. While we were tracking her movements, we didn't have a lot to go on. It all came out later. To start with, the Gallatin sheriff's department contacted Doc a couple of weeks after things had died down. They'd gotten some information from the Buffalo Trace Distillery—that's who she had been working for—that indicated she'd 'acquired' a bottle of Pappy from the counterfeiters the night before she was killed. They didn't say how, but it had to have come either from one of the bars or from the Willow Creek barn. Since she also had the empty bottle and the bag of marbles, Ockham would say it came from the barn."

"But how did the criminals find her?"

"There was CCTV surveillance at the Willow Creek property, at one of the bars, and at the Travelodge in Three Forks. This was obviously a sophisticated group, and it would not have been difficult for them to identify her. And they must have known she had more than just the bottle of whiskey. Of course, the sheriff also asked Doc if he knew anything about the Pappy, since it wasn't included the articles of hers that we'd returned to them. That really took some explaining, I can tell you; but fortunately, we had the Feds on our side by that time. They also gave us some additional background information."

"The Feds? What do you mean?"

"Don't worry. That's a detail I'll come to shortly."

"That's exactly what I want," I said. "Details."

Paying little attention to the speed limits—given the late hour, and the fact that this was, after all, Montana, famous for many years for *no* speed limits—it took LaFleur barely an hour and ten minutes to get to Pony. They were all waiting for him, Mary's phone on the bar in front of her.

There were four pictures, of varying quality. The first was of a stack of cartons, piled up to one side of the van's cargo space. The second picture was a closeup of one of the labels. The third and fourth pictures were even more surprising. "My God, how did you get these?" he asked.

"You don't really want to know," Mary said. "You're a worrier."

"You're right; I would probably feel I would have to lecture you again, and you've made it clear that is a waste of breath," he said, grinning. The proud smiles the three of them returned confirmed it.

"This is tremendous," LaFleur said as he confirmed that Mary's photos had been transferred to his phone successfully. "Mary," he then said carefully," I hate to have to ask you this, but can you tell me any more about Doug? Did the sheriff's department give you any details of how he died?"

"Just that it looked like he was shot at close range, and that Dr. Cady said the bullets appeared to have passed through his body. One in the face and one in the neck. They looked but couldn't find any bullets; they said they'd be back tomorrow if they could get some time away from the fires.

"So, I have something else for you, the real reason I asked you to come here," she said. "I know, I shouldn't have gone up there, but I couldn't stay away. I just had to see where he'd been killed. I walked back and forth up there, on the spot—I just ducked under the yellow Do Not Cross tape, I just had to be right there, somehow— and I walked back and forth, back and forth, just staring down at the ground, trying to understand." She held out two smooth, round marbles. "I found these, right where Doug had fallen. I think they're the same as those marbles in the picture I gave you."

These Don't Look Like Chinese Checkers to Me

DOC'S HOUSE

LaFleur's return to the house spurred quite a flurry of activity.

"These are the pictures from Mary," he told them. He brought the phone over to where Frank, Fuentes and Jamila could see what he was talking about. "She says she didn't have much time, but hopes these are useful."

The first was of the stacked cartons. LaFleur zoomed in trying to read the labels, but couldn't quite make out the printing.

The second picture was the closeup of a label. "How did she get these?" Fuentes asked.

"The same question I asked Mary. She wouldn't tell me all the details," LaFleur said, "but apparently they managed to lift the van driver's keys and keep him distracted while Mary climbed into the back."

"Wow," said Frank. "Impressive."

"They're quite a group."

As they read the contents, he turned to Jamila. "Any of this mean anything to you?"

"I'm thinking."

"Always a good thing." He brought up the next picture.

Jamila leaned in to take a closer look. "Aren't those the Chinese Checkers?" she asked.

"Yes. And I've also got—no, wait, first look at the last picture."

The fourth picture made them all sit up. It was well lit and crystal clear, and contained what LaFleur immediately sensed was the key. Laid out on the top of one of the cartons were three pieces of ceramic of varying configurations; one was a small, squarish block containing notches and slots of different sizes; one was a hollow tube with sharp, square protuberances at one end; and sitting next to the end of the tube was one of the small, round ceramic balls.

"Ah, Mary, you've turned out to be a real Mata Hari."

"Wasn't Mata Hari executed by the French?" asked Fuentes.

"Okay, bad comparison."

Jamila reached out towards LaFleur's hand. "May I take this for a few minutes?"

LaFleur didn't hesitate. "Certainly." He handed her the phone.

"There's more. Mary said she just couldn't stay away from the murder scene; she just had to see where it happened. She found these," he continued, pulling Mary's marbles from his pocket, "God knows how, on the spot where Doug was killed, after the body had been removed and the deputies had left the scene."

"Those look just like—"

"Yep, they're the same as the ones in Kyla's bag, just dirtied up a bit."

"How on earth did she get them?"

"Apparently the bullets passed though the body at a couple of points. She said she'd talked with Dr. Cady at the scene, so that's probably accurate."

Forty minutes later Jamila returned, setting her laptop down on the coffee table, turning it so LaFleur and Fuentes could see it, and also laying the bag of marbles down next to it. "Frank, you'll want to see this, too," she said, calling him over from the kitchen. He came in and stood behind them.

"Where's Maggie?" Jamila asked, looking around.

"Upstairs."

"Oh, right; we'll fill her in later. Okay, there is a lot going on here. We already know that they've got a 3-D printer operation going on; what we didn't know, until now, is what they are printing."

"Not just Christmas ornaments and paperweights."

"Right. Well, one item they are printing is almost as innocuous." She pointed over to the carry-on. "That empty bottle? Printed."

"Which makes sense. From what Ethan told me, empty Pappy bottles are readily available on eBay and such, but the Reserve bottles are available only in very limited quantities. They would need a larger source of bottles in order to create enough salable stock. Or if they planned to expand beyond Pappy into other, even rarer whiskies."

"Right."

"But I am also hearing that the bottles are not the main thing here."

"Right again. And this is where it gets really interesting." She brought up the close-up of the carton label. "I had to call a colleague back at RIT to find out exactly what this is. I had remembered her saying something about a poster session she'd seen at a materials conference a few months back. These appear to be cartons of high-grade graphene powder."

"What good is graphite for printing bottles?" asked LaFleur.

"It's not good for bottles at all; that just takes a simple polymeric silica compound. And it's not 'graphite,' but 'graphene.' Big difference. Graphene is a material derived from graphite, but an extremely unusual one, with extremely high tensile strength, but also extremely light weight. It's essentially a two-dimensional carbon crystal."

"Two-dimensional? That doesn't make sense. No material can be two-dimensional."

"It can if it's one atom thick." She shook her head. "But the technical details aren't important. What is important are the implications. What we've seen produced from their printer—aside from the bottle, which is just glass—appears to be ceramic. The so-called Chinese Checkers, the marbles, and the objects you saw in Pony, A.C.; while not commonly done on a commercial scale, 3-D printing of glass and ceramic is well understood. Graphene is typically produced in sheets, or deposited on various substrates, depending on the application. If they've developed a way to incorporate it into other materials for 3-D printing, that would be a tremendous breakthrough. The possibilities are endless."

"I don't care about the possibilities for the future of 3-D printing," said LaFleur, showing an unusual degree of impatience. "What does it mean for us? Right now?"

Jamila reached over and brought up Mary's fourth picture. "Okay, let's not worry about the graphene printing for the moment; it's important, but I'll get back to it later. This," she said, gesturing towards the photo, "looks to be—" She stopped suddenly and took a marble out of the baggie. "First let me tell you what I think these things are. These balls aren't Chinese Checkers, or marbles, or ball bearings, but based on the size—I don't have a micrometer with me, so I used a finely marked rule—my best estimate is a diameter slightly less than point-five inches. I then quickly checked some online sources, and found that the actual size is most likely point-four-eight-five inches. In other words, fifty caliber muzzle type ammunition." She pointed to the long, thin object in Mary's photo. "And that tube looks exactly the right size to be a gun barrel."

"So, what you're telling us," said Frank, slowly, "is that they are printing—"

"Guns," finished LaFleur. "And ammunition."

"And would they be detectable using x-rays?" asked Frank, quickly thinking ahead.

"No, they wouldn't. The material would be what is called 'radiolucent,' completely invisible to x-rays," answered Jamila. "And furthermore, using ceramic, especially if doped somehow with graphene, extremely durable." She held up a marble. "I smacked this with a hammer, and the hammer just bounced off. Didn't even leave a mark."

"And the guns would be much better than the single-use glass guns that are reportedly being printed now," said LaFleur. He looked at Frank. "You thinking what I'm thinking?"

"Reliable guns that could be printed anywhere, on demand."

"The perfect terrorist weapons."

At that moment, LaFleur's phone rang. "Hello, Mary. What is it?"

"Mr. LaFleur, we think something might be happening up here. After you left here, we saw a lot of activity up at the barn. It looks like they're packing up and getting ready to move out. And there's a black pickup parked at the house that we've never seen before either."

LaFleur stifled an exclamation of alarm. "A black pickup?"

"Yes. It arrived there just a little while ago."

"Mary, we've been expecting that pickup to show up at some point, and now that it has, you have got to get away from there. It's too dangerous for any of you to be anywhere near this thing now. If that driver had any idea that you were in that van—"

"Oh, no, Mr. LaFleur, we were very careful."

"No, Mary, it's too dangerous. I want you to get out of there and go home. You've done more than enough. Without your help, we wouldn't have had a chance of figuring this thing out. Please, all of you just get back to Harrison and stay safe."

"Well, okay, Mr. LaFleur. But you'll call if you need anything else, won't you?"

"Sure thing, Mary. And thank the boys for me."

LaFleur put away his phone and turned back to Jamila. "You were about to say something about incorporating graphene into various 3-D printed materials. Is that a big deal?"

"An extremely big deal. Like I said, as far as I know, graphene can only be fabricated for use in a very limited number of applications, mostly as depositions on various substrates. If this group has a way to incorporate true graphene into materials like these ceramic balls, it could revolutionize applied materials science."

"And their biggest concern is to flood the market with imitation Pappy Van Winkle?"

"Yeah, I know, it doesn't make a lot of sense."

"So, is the fake Pappy Van Winkel just a cover?" I asked, a bit incredulously. "And it's really all about printed guns?"

"Well, yes and no," replied LaFleur. "It's a bit more complicated than that. They really were interested in making money selling the fake Pappy, but it was probably more of a trial run. Just like rare wine, rare Scotch whisky sells at auction for astronomical prices. Sotheby's recently sold a bottle of The Macallan 1926 single malt—sixty years old, from a particular vat—for one and a half *million* pounds. That's almost two million dollars. A few years ago, a bottle of Glenfiddich sold at auction in Hong Kong for eighty-five thousand dollars. The presumption was that once they had the process down, and with the ability to manufacture their own bottles, remember, they could counterfeit any number of things. Champagne, for example, would be easy to make using a non-traditional method. High-end Krug, Dom Perignon, Armand de Brignac—these sell for tens of thousands of dollars a bottle, even a couple of hundred thousand. There's a big market out there.

"But more important, there was a lot more to the 3-D printing than just the guns. That operation, along with the whiskey scam, had apparently been intended as a side-line. Or maybe as an opportunistic funding operation. Terrorist operations at that time had shifted away from large-scale attacks to small, seemingly random incidents—stabbings on London Bridge, kamikaze cars running up onto the sidewalk, bar shootings, that kind of thing.

These guns would have been big sellers. But in any case, the real money was going to come later, from the graphene printing technology itself."

"Okay, that's another thing that has me puzzled. As soon as you mentioned it, I started to wonder—I mean, graphene composite is everywhere, isn't it? The Las Vegas Luna Hotel, the Channel Bridge, the New Dubai Pinnacle?"

"Sure, there's been an incredible explosion in graphene use in recent years, starting in about 2024. But this was ten years ago, in 2019. No one knew anything about it then."

"And yet this small group of penny-ante counterfeiters knew how to do it? How to create a graphene composite, something no one else had done?" *This is just too farfetched. There goes the Pulitzer.*

"Well, Reagan, as my dear friend Tamos Szabó used to say: all in good time."

Big Frank Gets His Black Ops On

DOC'S HOUSE

"Frank, can you meet me out on the deck?"

"Sure."

As they settled onto two of the large deck chairs, LaFleur looked out over the dark valley below to the Spanish Peaks, silhouetted in a reddish haze. "Fires seem to getting worse."

"Could be just a shift in wind direction."

"Hope they get things under control soon."

"What's up, A.C.?" Frank prompted.

"How safe do you think we are, Frank?"

"It depends on how much they know."

"Yes. And what do they know? Well, they knew that Kyla Macdonald had something on them. And they could reasonably assume that Doc had ended up with her suitcase, and that he may also have had some knowledge of what they were doing. But we've both been troubled by the extreme reaction at the loss of the suitcase—first the brazen public execution of Ms. Macdonald, then the double murder of Shorty Dalles and, as far as they know, Doc. Until very recently all we knew about them is that they are involved in the distribution of fake Pappy Van Winkle—which never seemed to be enough to warrant the drastic response. Now we know better."

"Because of what Mary found."

"And because they must believe that Kyla Macdonald had much more than just a bottle of their counterfeit whiskey. I don't believe that in itself would have been enough to drive them to multiple murders. Now we know we are not up against a simple counterfeiting ring, but are dealing with what appears to be an international syndicate of some kind, or even a terrorist organization. And the fact that this group, whoever they are, has somehow obtained access to leading edge technology, technology that Jamila didn't even know existed, has me very worried. With something like that potentially at stake, they are liable to take our interference very seriously, indeed. And now Doug Soames from Pony has been added to their list of victims.

"I didn't want to alarm the others, but I believe we are in very serious trouble here. Remember the other day, when Jamila said 'why don't we run?' My answer then was that we have no choice but to confront this thing head-on. But now I believe it's even more urgent. And that we are in more danger than I originally thought."

Frank stood up and walked to the deck rail and looked out over the dark pine woods below them, then turned back to LaFleur. "I agree. If it is truly as critical as that—and I believe it is—my instincts tell me that if they feel that threatened, they will do what I would do in their situation."

"Which is?"

"Kill us all."

LaFleur sat silently as Frank walked back over to his chair and sat down. "It's obvious they have no compunction about taking drastic measures," he continued. "They apparently know who we are, where we are, and what we most likely have in our possession. And they are going to want it back. And now that we have the intel from Mary, I believe that it will be soon. All of local law enforcement is swamped with these damned fires, and as skilled as the Moonlight Security staff is, they aren't prepared to deal with something like what I think we are facing.

"The first thing we need to do is get that suitcase away from the house. I should have stashed the evidence somewhere before now. Then I want to make sure the rest of the group is safe."

In the dim light, Frank could not see, but sensed, an imploring yet determined look in A.C.'s eyes.

"Frank, I think we could use some help."

Frank stood up, stretched his arms behind his back, above his head, then back down. He locked his hands together across his broad chest and threw his shoulders back, squaring himself with the world.

"Give me an hour." He turned and walked quickly back into the house.

It was actually slightly less than an hour later that Frank came into the living room and announced: "The Department of Homeland Security, along with agents from the ATF and FBI, will be staging at Ennis airport within the hour. As soon as we give the word, they'll transit to Moonlight by helicopter and use the Reserve helipad. I've already cleared it with Geno."

Sheltering in Place

"Okay, everyone please gather 'round." LaFleur waited for everyone to settle, then stood in the center of the room. "Things have escalated to the point where I no longer believe we are safe here. We have reason to believe that there could be movement out of Pony at any time. There are two things we need to do right away. One, I need to get the evidence away from here, somewhere safe. Doc suggested the Lodge; he's asked Ethan to come up with something.

"Two, I want you all out of the house. The Levine house to the west is currently vacant, Doc tells me; given our situation, and the special requirements we have—" he glanced upstairs— "it needs to be someplace close by. Frank will take charge of getting everyone moved over there, quietly and surreptitiously, while Doc and I are at the Lodge. We'll join you there as soon as we're done stowing the evidence."

At that moment, his phone chirping loudly and insistently.

"What the heck is that, A.C., an amber alert or something?" asked Maggie.

LaFleur had already pulled out his phone and was staring intently at the screen.

"*Jack Creek Road Incursion*, Frank. The F-150 must have just passed through the lower gate. They're on their way. Okay, everyone, we should have at least forty minutes to get things under control here."

"Oh, my God." It was Frank. LaFleur looked over at him in alarm—he'd never seen Frank look so distressed. He had actually gone pale.

"Jesus, Frank! What is it?"

"I've made a horrible mistake, A.C.," he said, practically choking out the words. "That incursion alarm—I told F.T. to set it up for the upper gate." He looked up at the ceiling, as if looking for guidance. "They're already practically in Moonlight."

"Son of a bitch!" LaFleur exploded. He put his hands to his face. "Son of a bitch," he repeated, softly this time. He took a deep breath. "Well, I certainly thought we'd have more time," he said, calmly.

"Okay, not your fault, Frank, and nothing to be done about it now. I should have made plans sooner. How soon can the Feds be here?"

"They said they can be on the Moonlight Reserve helipad in twenty minutes."

"Okay, call them. Let Geno know they're on the way." LaFleur had initially been surprised at how quickly Frank had managed to put together a deal with the Federal agencies, but then reminded himself that he shouldn't really be surprised at anything Frank did. He was deep, that one. This misstep was totally out of character. He knew Frank would never forgive himself if anything happened now.

"Doc, we've got to get the evidence out of here." Fuentes had taken the bottle of fake Pappy, the empty bottle, and the marbles—both the plastic bag of new marbles from Kyla's suitcase, and the two that Mary had supplied—and put it all in a canvas tote bag. The suitcase with the rest of Kyla's belongings was out in the garage; they'd planned to take it down to the sheriff as soon as possible.

"Okay, Doc, you're with me." A.C. said. "Frank will get the rest of you safely sheltered next door." He stopped and looked around. "Don't worry. We'll be back in a few minutes."

Unannounced House Guests

Frank had just come up from securing the basement doors, and Maggie had gone upstairs to get things there underway, when the doorbell rang. "Jamila! Are you downstairs?" she called.

"I'll get it," Jamila yelled back from the kitchen, as she went to the door.

The stranger peering through the crack in the partially open front door addressed Jamila in a heavy Slavic accent. "Good evening. Is Dr. Fuentes in?" Short and stocky, dressed expensively and somewhat inappropriately for the mountains, he had the air of a foreign ambassador arriving at a diplomatic function.

"No." She peered past the man in bewilderment, noticing that there was no car in the driveway, "I'm sorry, who are you?"

"That is no matter. I am here for Dr. Fuentes. Is he in?"

Before Jamila could answer, she was startled by noise from behind her. "What the hell!" she heard Frank exclaim. She stepped back a step to see what was happening, then stood frozen in alarm as a second stranger pushed his way into the house from the deck, closing the door behind him. He was dressed in a dark gray military-style uniform with no insignia or identifying marks. As he walked into the room, Frank immediately noticed his awkward, limping gait.

The man at the front door pushed his way in and moved purposefully into the foyer, shepherding Jamila and Frank into the living room in front of him.

Just then, Maggie came downstairs, calling out, "Is there anything wrong?" She stopped in confusion as she came into the room and saw the strangers there.

"Ah, one more," the man said, motioning for her to join the others. "Please, all of you, sit." The military man stepped forward and emphasized the order with the gun he was now holding in front of him. As they complied—Jamila and Maggie in helpless confusion, Frank controlled and deliberate—the man continued. "I am so sorry to impose," he said, his voice deep and fluid with an unmistakable undertone of threat. There was no question that he commanded the situation. Maggie and Jamila were ashen with shock, while Frank stared at the two intruders barely concealing an inner, helpless rage; his Glock was upstairs in the bedroom.

"I should tell you now," the man said, "I am fully aware of the unfortunate fact that Dr. Fuentes is not here. However, that is not my immediate concern. I am here for one reason only, something with which I am more than sure you can be of assistance." His formal manner and his careful, if accented, diction were unnerving, much more so than if he had acted belligerently. Maggie and Jamila sat quietly with eyes downcast, Frank still glaring.

"Is there anyone else in the house? Anyone upstairs?" the man asked, looking up in that direction.

"No, no one else is here," Frank replied.

He gave Frank a disappointed look. "Must I request my companion to search the house? The result could be quite disconcerting if you are lying."

"There's no need for that," said Maggie, quickly. "Like he said, there's no one else here."

"Well, you seem to be very sincere. I suppose I can take your word for this. It hardly matters. I am here for one thing. The suitcase. Give it to me, and I will go."

"What are you—" Frank began to say.

"Do not pretend to not know what I am talking about," the man said sharply. "The suitcase."

"It's not here." Frank tried to look sincerely apologetic.

The man motioned impatiently with a wave of his hand. "Oh, please. Just give it to me and we will go. I promise that no harm will come to you." He turned towards the other man. "Otherwise I am afraid that you will all die here, now, in this room."

"It's not here," said Maggie, desperation in her voice. "Really!"

"Oh, well then, where would it be?"

"It's been taken out of the house."

"By whom, may I ask?"

"By my husband."

"And who would that be?"

Maggie hesitated. The gunman prompted her with a wave of his pistol. "His name is LaFleur," she stammered, "A.C. LaFleur."

"And where, exactly, is this Mr. LaFleur, and what reason would he have to take it?"

"It's being turned over to the authorities."

The man shook his head and sighed theatrically. "I think you are lying." His voice dropped ominously. "Well, we can just kill you all now, I suppose." He turned to the man with the limp. "What do you think?" The man just shrugged, unconcerned. It was clearly a rhetorical question.

"Please, just let me call my husband," pleaded Maggie. "I'm sure that he can arrange something."

"Ah, so perhaps you are not lying?" He paused, as if weighing the options. "Very well, call him."

Into the Catacombs

MOONLIGHT LODGE

It took A.C. and Fuentes only a few minutes to get to the lodge. Not stopping at the front desk, Fuentes just called a "Hi, Justin" over his shoulder as they passed and went straight to the bar, where Ethan was presiding over an empty house.

"Where is everybody?" asked Fuentes, looking around.

"Evacuated. Haven't you heard? Fires are blocking highways all around us. Big Sky might be next."

"We've been busy," said A.C. "If that's the case, what are you still doing here?"

"Justin and I have been shutting things down. If you'd gotten here ten minutes later, we wouldn't have been here either."

"Okay, I'm glad we got here in time."

"Ethan, we need a place to stash this," Fuentes said, holding up the tote bag. "In a hurry."

"Catacombs," Ethan replied immediately.

"That sounds a bit frightening, but perfect," said A.C. "Where are they?"

"Follow me." Ethan led them to a door behind the bar. The catacombs turned out to be a large storage room, packed floor to ceiling with shelves and racks full of wine and liquor.

"Going to be hard to fit that bag in here inconspicuously," said LaFleur. He reached over and took the bottle of Pappy out of the bag and held it up. "Maybe we can just slip this in somewhere. What do you think, Ethan?"

Ethan looked around the room, then gestured to a shelf along one wall. "Over there," he said. He was pointing to about fifty bottles of Woodford Reserve bourbon, lined up two rows deep, all labeled with the name "Chris D'Hondt."

"That's a lot of Woodford," LaFleur said, taking a closer look. "What's the story behind the name on the label?"

"Those are all leftover from a rather extravagant birthday present."

"Some birthday!"

"Our members do it up right." Ethan indicated an area at the end of the row. "Slip your bottle in behind the Woodford, over there."

A.C. nodded and put the bottle of Pappy on the shelf, then came back over and pulled the marbles and the empty bottle out of the bag. "What about these?"

"Give them to me, A.C.," said Fuentes. "I've got an idea." He set the empty bottle on the floor and carefully poured the marbles from the plastic bag into it, then dropped Mary's two marbles—bullets, he silently corrected himself—into the bottle as well. Then he stuck it on the shelf behind the bottle of Pappy. "Not perfect, but there's no way anyone will find it in here."

"I'll lock the door behind us," said Ethan.

"Okay, Ethan, thanks a lot. Now we need to get out of here."

They had barely made it to the front door when LaFleur's phone rang.

It was bad news.

"Maggie?"

"A.C., listen," said Maggie, breathlessly. "There is someone here, two men, threatening to kill us unless they get the suitcase."

"Son of a bitch!" He held the phone away from his mouth and whispered to Fuentes, "They are already at the house." He came back to Maggie. "Let me talk to them, to whoever is in charge." A moment later, he heard the deep, accented voice.

"Mr. LaFleur. I understand you have something that belongs to me. I want it."

"It's not yours, whoever you are. You killed the woman it belonged to."

"I will be more precise. There are items in that suitcase that belong to me. I will have them back, or the unfortunate souls here in this house will suffer greatly. I am serious about this. Bring the suitcase here immediately."

LaFleur cast his eyes about the room, thinking desperately. "Meet me here, in the bar at the Moonlight Lodge; leave my friends out of it. I'll deal with you directly, turn it over, but only here."

"And why should I do this? You don't seem to realize, Mr. LaFleur, that I hold all of the cards. Besides, why should I be so foolish as to come to a public place?"

"It'll be just us; the Lodge is empty due to the fires. There are no guests and the staff have all left under pre-evacuation orders."

"Still, why do I not just kill your friends now and then come and take it from you?"

"Because if you do that, you'll never get what you want. I can be away from here in thirty seconds. I know these mountains; you do not. You will not only lose what you want, I will turn everything over to the authorities long before you could catch up to me. Just leave my people alone and get over here and we can still make a deal. All I want at this point is to protect my friends." He broke the connection.

He turned to Fuentes. "Two men have the group at the house, threatening to kill them unless I bring the stuff to them. I told him they have to come here."

"Jesus!"

"Don't worry. I should hear back from him any minute. It's clear that if I can't get them here on my terms, we're all dead anyway, now or later. As long as we are dealing with just two of them, we have a chance. But it has to be here."

LaFleur's phone rang. "Yes?"

"We will be there in ten minutes."

A.C. put the phone back in his pocket and looked around. "Ethan, do you keep any weapons here?"

"We keep a pistol at the front desk, a .45, for bears. And there's a deer rifle in one of the back offices."

"Please get the pistol for me, Ethan." Ethan returned a minute later carrying a large pistol in a worn leather holster. LaFleur pulled it out and examined it quickly. "Just the thing," he said, replacing it in the holster and looking around. "But I'll need some place to hide it, someplace I can still get to it in a hurry."

"I've got just the thing," Ethan said. "There are hooks under the bar," he said, pointing. "You know, for women to hang a purse on, things like that."

LaFleur leaned over and looked intently at the underside of the bar. "I'll be damned. That will work." He hung the pistol up out of sight.

Fuentes in the meantime had been standing by in something of a daze. "Jesus, A.C.," he said again.

"Oh, Doc," A.C. said, as if just realizing that Fuentes was still there. "Get out of sight, will you? They think you're dead, remember? And Ethan, you and Justin get out of here, pronto."

"Just one thing left to do, Mr. LaFleur," he said, going back behind the bar. LaFleur watched in amazement as Ethan quickly but carefully made a Famous Grouse floater and set it on the bar.

"Thanks, Ethan. Now, get out!" Ethan hurried out of the bar, calling to Justin as he got to the lobby. "Time to go!"

"Leave the door unlocked!" LaFleur called after them. "And you, Doc, get upstairs, lock yourself in a room, or something."

Fuentes looked back at him, almost in anguish. "But, A.C., I can't just—"

"What you can't do is stay here."

With that, Fuentes straightened up, nodded silently, and hurried out of the bar and up the main staircase.

Just as LaFleur heard a door close upstairs, he heard the huge front door of the lodge swing open and closed. *Good, Ethan and Justin are out of harm's way.* He settled onto the stool in Poet's Corner and took a small sip of the floater. Then he reached down and reassured himself that the pistol was really hanging there under the bar.

Time to play out the hand.

Billy Ockham Buys a Round

MOONLIGHT LODGE

The two men who came around the corner behind the hostages looked as if they meant business. LaFleur had been right to worry. Which was no consolation at this point.

The shorter, stockier man was dressed well, almost elegantly, and was obviously in charge; the other one, taller and moving with an odd gait, was just as clearly the gunsel, even if his gun had not been clearly visible.

The first man motioned to his charges to sit at the bar, along what LaFleur had heard Ethan refer to as "Mahogany Ridge." The two women looked frightened but composed; Frank moved smoothly and alertly, sitting on the edge of his stool, the balls of his feet resting tautly on the floor in front of him.

As the assassin—as LaFleur and Frank had immediately pegged him—stood off to the side, gun trained on the group at the bar, the man in charge stepped forward, carefully adjusting his tie, smoothing down the front of his dark suit jacket, until he stood opposite LaFleur. He clasped his hands behind his back.

LaFleur studied the man's pose, the drape of his coat, the smooth crease of his pants. He could see no indication that he was concealing a gun. He was the type who invariably had someone else do the hard work. Just as he'd hoped, it would be one on one. "Well, you must be Mr. LaFleur," the man said.

"And you are?"

"Oh, just for the fun of it, why don't you call me Boris," the man answered with a smile.

"I guess that will have to do."

Boris stopped smiling and leaned forward slightly. "You have something of mine. I will have it back."

"Not while my friends are being threatened."

"Perhaps you do not understand the situation you are all in. You really have no choice."

"There is always a choice. And I've made mine. I have what you want and you don't know where it is, or what might happen to it if I'm not around to make sure it stays hidden. You should know I'm not dumb enough to come in here without having made arrangements. In any case, the ATF is on their way here as we speak. You'd better turn my friends over to me; it's going to be hard on you."

The group at the bar began to show signs of distress. Maggie and Jamila were breathing hard and staring down at the bar; Frank, while trusting that LaFleur had some sort of plan, still could not keep the anxious look off his face.

"Oh, really, Mr. LaFleur," said Boris, breezily, "do not try to bluff me. You don't understand what a really weak hand you hold. Let the ATF come. It is just a minor liquor violation; I'll pay the fine."

"Now you're the one trying to bluff. There's more to it than that," said LaFleur.

"I am quickly losing patience. You know I will kill you all."

"Over a liquor violation?" *I need more time.*

"Oh, you know there's more to it, you just said so. No, this is the end. Sorry, I have all the aces this time. We killed the meddling woman investigator, we killed the patsy from the sporting goods store, we killed the poor rube from Pony, we killed Fuentes, and now we are going to kill you, and all of your friends, sad to say, whom you have brought into this. Very sad." He turned to the assassin. "Kill that man first. He looks dangerous."

Frank visibly tensed, but did not move.

LaFleur sat at the bar silently, hands clenched in anticipation of what he knew he had to do, any second now. *Where are the Feds?*

As the assassin raised his pistol then slowly lowered it to point directly at Frank, a voice suddenly came from behind them.

"Not so fast."

"Who is that?" Boris asked, straining to see into the dim light.

"The guy you had killed," they all heard, as Fuentes stepped out into the light. "Dr. Michael Fuentes, at your service."

LaFleur scarcely glanced at Fuentes as he shifted on his stool, with only the barest thought given to what the hell Fuentes thought he was doing here, every muscle in his body primed to act.

"Fuentes?" Boris turned to the assassin, enraged. "You idiot! You said he was dead! Stupid idiot!" he screamed, raising his fist near the assassin's face. Given his previous calm demeanor, it was surprising how quickly he'd lost his composure. Flinching involuntarily, the assassin's gun wavered ever so slightly and his eyes flickered fractionally away from his target.

LaFleur reached down and drew the pistol from its holster under the bar, firing quickly on the way up, just as the assassin fired wildly into the air. The resulting report echoed through the bar as the assassin fell violently backwards. His gun skidded across the floor as his body landed with a dull thud.

There was a loud commotion out in the lobby as the government team swept into the lodge: two agents each from the FBI and the ATF, the lead agent from DHS, all followed by Matt. And that was not all—as they entered the bar, another figure walked forward from the shadows.

Mike Wilcynski, blood running down his face from under the gauze wrapping his head, stepped slowly forward with a rifle in his hands. As they all stood gaping, he collapsed to the floor.

The FBI and ATF agents gathered up the evidence like a swarm of locusts—the spent cartridges were collected and stored, "Boris" was unceremoniously handcuffed and led away, and the assassin disappeared in a black body bag. The DHS agent warned all present that everything they had witnessed, heard about, or even speculated on was strictly off limits—any indication that word had been leaked concerning 3-D printing of firearms, or for that matter, any mention of 3-D printing at all, could result in severe extrajudicial actions against LaFleur, Frank, and Mike Wilcynski, and anyone else they thought could be a security threat. Moonlight Security would also be vigorously debriefed.

A second team had been dispatched by helicopter from Bozeman immediately at the time of the Lodge confrontation, and moved in on the operation at North Willow Creek twenty minutes later. They took it down without a fight.

Maggie and Jamila had not moved from their stools at the bar, watching the activity swirl around them as if they were suddenly thrust into the middle of a Jack Ryan movie, bewildered and relieved at their salvation. Frank, true to form, had immediately jumped up and began instructing the FBI in proper crime scene procedures. To their credit, and Frank's, they listened respectfully. Of course, the fact that he and the DHS agent were old friends didn't hurt.

Mike got another ride to the hospital, again with no lights and siren—the bleeding was minor, and he'd collapsed to the floor in a state of relieved shock rather than from any medical trauma. Fuentes sat by his side the entire way.

The Man Who Shot Liberty Valence

"You devils!" I slammed my hand down on the table in a flash of surprised anger, causing the drinks on the table to jump. Looking back and forth to A.C. and Doc sitting across from me, seeing the looks on their faces, I couldn't help but burst into laughter. "You cagey devils!"

We had all gathered at the Moonlight Lodge bar at my request for a post-mortem of sorts, and as a last attempt for me to get the final story—my deadline was approaching and I was beginning to think I would end up with something half finished. *Pulitzer, ha!*

A.C. and Maggie had come out to Moonlight for an extended stay, this time without smoke and fire everywhere. And no one shooting at anyone, at least not in the local vicinity. Frank was off on one of his "jaunts," as LaFleur called it, trekking through Cambodia, Laos, and Vietnam. He'd wanted to "see what the place was like without someone shooting at me," he'd told LaFleur. Jamila had had to return to SUNY for the Fall semester and was also sorely missed.

I sat there shaking my head. "I just can't believe it! All this time you let me believe that Mike Wilcynski was dead!"

"Well, it seemed only right, since we'd let everyone in Big Sky think the same thing for over a week," said LaFleur, obviously trying to hold holding back his amusement at my reaction.

"But what about his family?" I couldn't help thinking, *how callous*!

"They were off in the wilds of Portugal, remember? We'd tried to contact them, but apparently that area of Portugal has about the same level of cell phone service we get around here," said Doc.

"But still, wasn't Mike pretty severely wounded?"

"Nope. Well, I guess that depends on what you mean by 'severe.' Compared to being dead, of course, Mike was very lucky—just a significant concussion and the accompanying symptoms; headache, dizziness, nausea. The trip to the hospital when he was shot was taken slowly to minimize the trauma; since I knew the wound was not life-threatening it seemed unnecessary. At the hospital they did an MRI and discharged him to my care. As it turned out, it also helped in the subterfuge."

"Because there was no record of Doc being admitted to the hospital—just Mike, who they wouldn't connect with the attempt."

"Exactly."

"And since the assassin had seen someone on the course with the right hat, the unmistakably ugly hat, and didn't know Mike's name, the inference would have been natural. He used Ockham's Razor but was outrageously wrong."

"That's right," said LaFleur. "The double switch was too much for him. First the bag and then the hat."

"And there was yet another switch," I said. "Mike for Doc."

"And once we knew Mike was going to be okay, we decided we had better use that to the best advantage we could. That's why we kept him hidden upstairs at Doc's house, being nursed by Maggie. And Doc also kept himself out of sight, at least after that first trip to the golf club."

"That had us worried," said Doc. "We were afraid they'd go back to the club and try to verify my death. But Frank is so clever— we call him 'Clever Hans,' sometimes—he'd come up with the idea of planting my obituary in the Oswego paper, the Palladium-Times. And our computer hacker had also inserted a bogus entry into the Madison County coroner database listing my demise. That must have fooled them."

"I thought that the obituary was a bit overboard," said LaFleur, "and it did alarm Doc's friends back in Oswego. But fortunately, that's a very small group."

"Very funny."

"But it worked. They were convinced that I'd been killed, and that particular risk of exposure had been covered. And that might have been the end of the killing, if only Doug Soames hadn't been so damned curious." Fuentes looked around and noticed that the drinks around the table were close to being depleted. He raised his arm and called to Ethan.

"Yes, Doc?" Ethan called from the bar.

"Another round, please, sir!" Doc called back.

I picked up my glass and drained the last dregs. "Kyla sure knew her stuff, huh, Doc?"

"That's why it's on the drink menu now," he replied. "A.C., did you see this?" He asked, picking up the menu and holding it out for LaFleur to look at. "There on the right side: Poor Girl's Pappy."

"Well, what do you know. Good for her!"

"Ethan says they're very popular. A few of the locals have even taken up my shorthand for it: PGP."

I sat back while Ethan served the drinks, feeling a bit overwhelmed. All of this new information was—what's the old expression? It was like drinking from a fire hose. But it was all finally beginning to make sense.

I picked up my notebook and flipped back a few pages; there was something else that had been bothering me. "There's another thing that I didn't get," I said. "How was it that Frank was able to get DHS, ATF, the FBI, all there so quickly?"

"That's our Frank," said LaFleur, chuckling. "Actually, it turned out that they had been tracking this Boris character's movement for quite some time. Frank's department connection was at a high enough level that he was able to arrange their cooperation quickly—in fact, they'd been looking for just such an opportunity. His real name, by the way, is Ivan Nikolayevich Lubchenko, a rather notorious Belarusian oligarch."

"And the 3-D printing? How on earth did they get access to a technology that was at that time still in its infancy?"

"That's the really interesting part of all of this," said LaFleur. "The guns, as we've said before, were simply an expedient way to make some quick cash. The counterfeit Pappy, and the plans for additional fakes, likewise. Strictly opportunistic. The real deal was the graphene composite printing. That's what the Feds wanted hushed up. Not just because of the terrorist angle, but because of the immense impact it could have had on the global markets. Several governments had been working on the development of this technology, but no one so far had come up with a viable product. Except one."

"And?" I practically jumped across the table.

"As so often is the case," said Doc, "it was an independent researcher in an out of the way back water that made the breakthrough. A doctoral student, no less, at an obscure laboratory at the University of Belgrade, Serbia—formerly Yugoslavia, for those keeping score—who had come up with a method of incorporating almost pure graphene with other materials."

"But why didn't he publish his results, get credit for the discovery?"

"Because he was Lubchenko's first victim."

"From what we can infer," said LaFleur, falling back on Ockham one last time, "Lubchenko found out about it, by whatever means, and he wanted to make sure that no one else had any knowledge of it. The student was found incinerated in his laboratory. No one was ever arrested for what was obviously arson."

"How is that possible? Wasn't there an investigation?"

"Oligarchs have long arms."

"But the process is well known now," I said. "How did that come about?"

"Everything was in the van, all of the detailed specifications for the exact process they had been using. Once the government realized what they had, for once they did the right thing and released the information. The university in Belgrade is receiving royalties on the process from companies all over the world to this day."

"And one other good thing came out of it," said Doc. "The printer itself—after the Feds had completed their forensic examination—was donated to the high school in Harrison. Mary was the driving force behind that; she's related to a Montana Senator, and he was able to make it happen. So, thanks to Mary, Harrison High was one of the first schools in Montana to have a 3-D printer."

I sat back, trying to take it all in. I put down my pen and laid my notebook to one side. Ethan brought over a round of drinks. It was at this moment that LaFleur started to whistle. Off key, but recognizable. A tune from a famous film score. I looked at him imploringly. "What—?"

"There's one last detail you need to know," LaFleur said, rising from the table. He walked over to the bar, to Poet's Corner. "Reagan, there's something here I want to show you."

I went to the bar and watched in some bemusement as A.C. pulled the bar stool away from the corner.

"Here's where I was sitting that night," he said. "Lean down and take a look under the bar."

I bent down and peered under the edge of the bar. "What am I looking for?"

He leaned over and ran his finger along the underside of the bar. "Ah, there it is," he said. "Look closely, Reagan, and you'll see a bullet lodged in the wood."

I looked closely at the point he'd found, and saw the dull gray slug embedded deeply in the bar. "I see it," I said, still not quite getting it.

"That's the bullet I fired from my pistol. I didn't shoot the assassin. I damn near shot myself in the foot."

"But then—"

"That's right. It was Mike."

EPILOGUE

The house sat on a narrow lot on a quiet, wooded street in the Hyde Park area of Cincinnati, an older, red brick two-story with a large center dormer and a front porch with a white spindled railing. There was a low stone wall bordering the front lawn, and flower beds flanking a short set of steps up from the sidewalk and at the front and sides of the house. There was a small American flag displayed in the front window. It was not far from Woodbridge School, a private school for children with learning disabilities that Kyla Macdonald's daughter Ailsa was now attending.

LaFleur had spoken to Kyla's mother that morning to arrange the visit. As he stood on the porch waiting for her to answer the door, he rehearsed once more what he was going to say her, and to Ailsa; how he was going to explain what had happened.

Kyla's mother opened the door and asked him in. Standing near the back of the parlor, next to a long stairway and gripping the polished oak bannister, was a nine-year-old girl with coppery-blonde hair, green eyes, and a shy smile.

Ailsa's grandmother gently urged Ailsa into the room, and stood by her, her hand resting on the girl's shoulder. LaFleur held out his bag of presents, the presents Kyla had left at the Three Forks motel.

Ailsa reached out her hand, eyes shining. "Mama's presents," she said.

LaFleur forgot everything he was going to say.

ACKNOWLEDGMENTS

As always, we owe a debt of gratitude to our loyal reviewers, who have spent many hours poring over drafts, and who have saved us from many egregious errors. Those errors still remaining (and we do not doubt that there are a few) are, of course, entirely ours.

First and foremost, Sandy Fountain and Adrienne Abbott were not only extremely helpful, but understanding, as usual. We couldn't do this without their help.

Our other assistants include (but may not be limited to, and if we have missed you, we apologize): Otis and Joy Kramer; Nick and Jill Page; Gerard and Kerry McMahon; Pete Huisveld; Sarah Massey-Warren; Marcia Volin; Debbie Abbott; Randy and Melanie Palmer; Geoff Chase; Vicki Key; Barb Kok; Sandy Carlson; Ken Nagel; and Dr. Mike Luckow.

We must also thank all of our friends in Moonlight and Madison County for so generously allowing us to use them as models (not always accurately) for many of the characters in the novel: Mary, Reagan, Mike, Geno, Matt, Chris, Greg, Nick, Ethan, Lat, and the many more who made "cameo" appearances: many thanks to you all.

Made in the USA
Monee, IL
16 January 2024

51296898R00085